R.5,

What the critics are saying...

ဆ

5 cups "With highly sensual and erotic sex scenes, your senses will be set afire." ~ *Coffee Time Romance*

4.5 stars "If you like hotter than hot, this is your story." ~ *Romantic Times Book Reviews,.*

5 gleaming angels and a Recommended Read! "Scorching hot, passionate, dynamic." ~ *Fallen Angel Reviews,*

To Trust a Wolf

Kate Steel

ELLORA'S CAVE
ROMANTICA PUBLISHING

An Ellora's Cave Romantica Publication

www.ellorascave.com

To Trust a Wolf

ISBN 1419953753
ALL RIGHTS RESERVED.
To Trust a Wolf Copyright © 2005 Kate Steele
Edited by Heather Osborn
Cover art by Syneca

Electronic book Publication February 2005
Trade paperback Publication August 2006

Excerpt from *Lions and Tigers and Bears* Copyright © Jodi Lynn Copeland, Kit Tunstall, Kate Steele, 2005.

Excerpt from *Weather Ballons Make Rotten Sex Toys* Copyright © Annabelle du Fouet, 2004

Warning:

The following material contains graphic sexual content meant for mature readers. This story has been rated E–rotic by a minimum of three independent reviewers.

Ellora's Cave Publishing offers three levels of Romantica™ reading entertainment: S (S-ensuous), E (E-rotic), and X (X-treme).

S-*ensuous* love scenes are explicit and leave nothing to the imagination.

E-*rotic* love scenes are explicit, leave nothing to the imagination, and are high in volume per the overall word count. In addition, some E-rated titles might contain fantasy material that some readers find objectionable, such as bondage, submission, same sex encounters, forced seductions, and so forth. E-rated titles are the most graphic titles we carry; it is common, for instance, for an author to use words such as "fucking", "cock", "pussy", and such within their work of literature.

X-*treme* titles differ from E-rated titles only in plot premise and storyline execution. Unlike E-rated titles, stories designated with the letter X tend to contain controversial subject matter not for the faint of heart.

Also by Kate Steele

ઋ

Chosen of the Orb
Lions and Tigers and Bears
Planetary Passions: Venus Connection
The Orb of Atrios

About the Author

ઋ

Having been an avid reader of romance for years, and being possessed of an overactive imagination, Kate decided only recently to try her hand at writing. She discovered that, like reading, writing romance has become addictive. Whether writing about werewolves and otherworldly creatures or contemporary gay/erotic romance, she has found the perfect outlet and is thrilled to be part of the Ellora's Cave family.

Kate lives in a turn-of-the-century house located on three acres in the midst of Indiana farm country. Keeping her company is her family, dogs, and other assorted pets.

Kate welcomes comments from readers. You can find her website and email address on her author bio page at www.ellorascave.com

To Trust a Wolf

ഇ

Dedication

My sincere thanks to my editor, Heather, for believing in this, my first book accepted for publication and for working so hard to make it shine.

Chapter One

ဢ

"I'm through with men," Bryn Roydan stated.

"I take it your date didn't work out last night?" her friend Clare Harrelson asked sympathetically.

Bryn and Clare were co-owners of the Whispering Springs Book Shop and as close as sisters. They'd been fast friends since their first meeting in the fifth grade. A dodgeball game, legendary in the minds of an awed bunch of eleven year olds, had ended in a standoff between the two of them. Thus began their long and enduring friendship.

Taking a break from their flourishing business, the ladies were ensconced in a high-backed booth at the best eatery in town, O'Neal's. The place was packed. Waitresses raced back and forth with menus and food as a steady stream of customers ebbed and flowed with the lunch rush.

"It was a disaster," Bryn replied in answer to Clare's query about her date. She tossed back a lock of tawny blonde hair. "We went to Antonia's for pizza before the movie. He ate like a pig."

"Exactly how like a pig?" Clare asked, her fork poised over a juicy slice of tomato.

"You know how some people can eat with their fingers and be neat about it? Not him. He got sauce and stuff all over his hands. It was just gross!" Bryn declared with a dramatic shudder.

Clare smiled indulgently. "Aren't you being a little fastidious?"

"Wait 'til you hear the rest!" Bryn exclaimed with a disgusted frown. "We went to see that new fantasy movie. You know, the one made from those popular children's books? Well, he put his arm around me. Thank god he washed his hands before we left Antonia's. Anyway, he kept drumming his fingers on my shoulder. And he wouldn't shut up! He made stupid comments about their British accents and kept trying to imitate them."

Bryn was on full vent mode.

"Then he says to me, 'you should be in this movie'. Of course, like an idiot I say why and he says—get this— 'you're as lovely as a fantasy'. Eewww!!! Is that the lamest thing you've ever heard in your life?"

"Oh, I don't know, I think it's kinda sweet," Clare answered with mock sincerity while batting her eyelashes.

Bryn pinned Clare with a frowning glare. Amusement sparked in Clare's eyes and an answering spark lit in Bryn's as both of them began snickering.

Clare reached for her water. "So what did you say?"

"I told him he was silly and excused myself to go to the restroom so I could barf." At Clare's raised eyebrow Bryn confessed, "Okay, I didn't barf, even though I felt like it." Bryn sat back with a sigh. "After the movie he asked me if I'd like to stop somewhere for dessert. But the thought of seeing him eat again? No way."

"So he took you home and…?" Clare prompted.

"And he kissed me. It was like kissing a trout. Yuck!" Bryn's grimace of distaste had Clare smiling again. "Clare, you are so lucky to have Brian."

"Honey, you don't have to tell me that." A tender look filled Clare's eyes as she thought of her husband.

When they met in college, Brian had been an English major. He was tall, with dark brown hair, and his eyes always seemed to reflect a serene, tranquil expression. He was studious and quiet, not in a nerdy way, but in a calm, sure, masculine manner. Marrying after graduation, they moved to Brian's hometown, Whispering Springs, Minnesota.

Bryn was genuinely happy for Clare and Brian. They had the relationship that she had hoped for when she'd married four years ago. All during college she'd had one boyfriend and then another, never finding anyone she felt any real attachment to, until she met her ex-husband during the last months of her senior year. Bryn held a part-time office job and he was a computer consultant, hired to upgrade the system of the company for which she worked. They'd spent some time chatting during business hours while he worked with the upgrades and when he asked her out, she accepted with real pleasure. He had at first reminded her of her father. He had a great sense of humor and a gregarious personality. They'd enjoyed the proverbial whirlwind romance and Bryn had found herself swept away with emotions the likes of which she'd never experienced before. After a short engagement and a small wedding attended by family and friends ten months after meeting him, Bryn found herself in the role of wife.

All too soon his resemblance to her father paled and disappeared. Bryn eventually found out that he lacked any loyalty or honor. Too late she discovered his self-serving attitude and his blatant disregard for his marriage vows. He revealed himself to be insecure and bigoted. The sense of humor she took such delight in at first turned wicked and cruel.

The sexual aspect of their relationship had never been earthshaking. At first he'd been eager and attentive, and even though the act itself seemed to go so quickly she never quite managed to reach orgasm, she told herself she was content because she loved him.

And she had loved him deeply, despite his personality flaws. Which was why, when she discovered he was having an affair after only two years of marriage, she was totally devastated.

Realizing her marriage was a farce, Bryn obtained a divorce. Needing a change, she'd quickly agreed when Clare urged her to move to Whispering Springs. They had always talked about opening a bookstore together, and it seemed the perfect time. Bryn found herself starting over in a new town, with her best friend as her business partner.

Lost in their separate thoughts, Bryn and Clare gave themselves a mental shake and smiled at each other. "Well, I'm through," Bryn reiterated. "My judgment, as far as men are concerned, is definitely flawed. From now on I'm sticking with my vibrator." She paused thoughtfully. "Although you know, even that's beginning to lose its appeal. Do you think it's possible to be over-vibrated? I think my clit was getting numb the other night."

Clare whooped with laughter, slapping a hand over her mouth when the faces of some of the other diners turned her way. "Oh my god, Bryn, I can't believe you said that!"

"Don't you dare tell Brian," she demanded, her face flushing as she watched Clare blot tears of laughter with a napkin. "I don't know what's wrong with me anymore. Maybe my ex-husband was right. Maybe I am frigid."

"Now wait a minute," Clare began, pausing as the waitress, who'd brought their check, asked if they'd like dessert. After replying with a negative she continued, "Are you going to sit there and tell me you're going to believe the word of a guy who you describe as having a four-inch dick and five-minute time limit?"

Bryn pursed her lips, considering the question. "Well…I guess not. But there must be something wrong with me," she offered. "Guys I think are special turn out to be frogs. And I've never been able to orgasm while having sex with a man. I don't think I can even come anymore without a vibrator."

Seeing her friend's distress, Clare began quietly, "Bryn, honey, how many men have you had sex with?"

"You already know the answer to that," Bryn answered, meeting Clare's steady look. "Two."

"Right. One high-school sweetheart. A teenage boy who didn't know the first thing about sex. And then a self-serving, womanizing asshole who wouldn't take the time and probably didn't have the skill to satisfy his own wife." Placing her hand over Bryn's, she continued, "Baby, you just haven't met the right guy. You need somebody mature and confident. Somebody like, say…Logan Sutherland?"

Bryn's eyes widened in apprehension. "Oh, no. No, no. He scares the hell out of me," she exclaimed. "He's so big, and gorgeous and…and big," she repeated helplessly. "Besides, you know I turned him down when he asked me to have dinner with him." She shook her head decisively. "He'll never ask me again."

"As I recall, he asked, you said you were busy and he said perhaps another time, to which you replied yes. That, I believe, was an invitation to please ask again," Clare pointed out triumphantly.

"Even if he does ask I'll have to say no," Bryn asserted.

"For heaven's sake, why?" Clare asked incredulously. "If a man like that asked me out, I'd have to take a minute to remember I'm a happily married woman."

Bryn studied the bill and calculated the tip. Digging into her purse for money, she paused. "I feel kind of stupid saying this, but there's something dangerous about that man."

"Bryn, honey, you're letting your imagination run wild." Clare studied her friend thoughtfully. "Could be that 'danger' you feel is a threat to your peace of mind."

"And my heart," Bryn muttered resentfully. "Logan Sutherland is not the type of man who will walk away and leave a woman's heart intact."

"And what makes you so sure he'll walk away?" Clare challenged.

"I could never hope to hold the interest of a man like him," Bryn sighed.

Clare shook her head. "You have a very bad habit of selling yourself short. And you're assuming an awful lot about someone you don't really know. Go out with him once and see what happens. And as to whether or not you hold his interest?" She reached out and tapped Bryn on the nose. "Why don't you let him be the judge of that?"

Wrinkling her nose, Bryn said nothing as she and Clare slid out of their booth to head back to work.

* * * * *

Seated in the high-backed booth directly behind the one Bryn and Clare had just vacated, Logan Sutherland thoughtfully sipped his iced tea. "Yes, Bryn," he murmured, "Why don't you let me be the judge of that?"

Logan was thirty-three and a big man. Tall, strong, muscular. Sable brown hair, with a natural wave, brushed the tops of his shoulders and shone with reddish-gold highlights. His golden brown eyes were set in a ruggedly handsome face. Calmly serene at the moment, those same eyes, in times of stress, passion or anger, would change to a glowing amber-gold.

Drawing in a deep breath, Logan's senses filtered through the various scents filling the restaurant until he found the one for which he searched. Bryn.

She never wore perfume. He savored the natural, warm, fresh scent of her. Lids closed over eyes that began to gleam with a rich, golden light. A contented smile ghosted across sculpted male lips. There certainly were advantages to being a werewolf. Enhanced sense of smell being one.

Logan was not inexperienced when it came to women. He enjoyed them, reveled in them when and where his needs arose. Most of his partners were lupine females, some few had been human, but all were given the unmistakable understanding that their involvement was temporary. He'd been more than satisfied with this arrangement until Bryn arrived.

Being acquainted with Brian and Clare, he'd heard firsthand Clare's enthusiastic plans for the bookstore she and her friend Bryn were going to open. Clare had enthused over Bryn's pending arrival, and how she hoped the new business would help her friend get over her painful divorce. A voracious reader himself, Logan had promised to be there for the grand opening.

When the big day arrived, Logan entered the store with all the other eager patrons. They were greeted with pristine shelves of books, those wonderful purveyors of knowledge and entertainment.

Several nooks with sofas or tables and chairs had been set up in various locations around the store for the customers' comfort and enjoyment. The smell of fresh-brewed coffee wafted through the air.

For Logan, a scent of a much more intriguing nature had drawn his attention. Female. An alluring, subtle fragrance that was bewitching. He literally followed his nose as it led him to Bryn.

At the sight of her, certain parts of his anatomy began to behave in a most unruly fashion. The inner wolf began a low, rumbling growl that quickly became a howl, declaring his intent to claim his mate. Logan had struggled to hold his animal at bay. His mate. There was no mistaking that delicious, compelling scent. Clare, catching sight of Logan, had motioned him over and made the introductions.

Although friendly, Bryn had exhibited a certain wariness, as though privy to his plans. Aware of her past, Logan had reined in his impatience, keeping the conversation casual, making no overt moves that would startle or alarm her. He was determined to give her time to get used to him. He understood the value and virtue of patience. With that in mind he'd made his excuses and left, promising himself the pleasure of repeated visits.

Now, as he finished off his lunch, Logan thought about all the interesting things he had overheard. Was it his fault that his hearing was particularly acute?

While her description of her date had been amusing, Logan had found his body going taut with rage at the thought of another man touching that which he considered his. The time had come to make his claim. First he would put her fear of him to rest. Then he would show her all the pleasure a proper mate could bring.

Bryn's vibrator was about to be retired.

* * * * *

Logan returned home to find trouble there ahead of him.

"Are you listening to me, Logan?"

Staring absently out the window as the conversational buzz continued over the speakerphone, he relaxed in the snug, familiar atmosphere of his den. A warm, mid-August breeze stirred the leaves of the maples that shaded the house as it flowed into the open windows.

Drapes billowed against cream-colored walls, which lightened the influence of dark oak wainscoting. A long, wide sofa upholstered in soothing greens and muted gold sat perpendicular to the fireplace. Facing it was a coffee table and two matching overstuffed chairs. Logan's heavy oak desk sat in one corner, presiding over the room. Backed by shelves filled with books, it was the center of Logan's work area.

Straightening in his chair, he swiveled around to face the phone. "I'm listening, Jace, and I really don't see the problem. Twin Pines pack wants recompense. You admit it's owed. Pay it. End of story."

"That's just it, Logan, that's not the end of the story. I got a call this morning from that Twin Pines beta bitch, Lillian. They not only want recompense, they want a show of submission from Iron Tower pack. Specifically from Iron Tower's alpha." A low growl rumbled through the phone line. "I will not bare my throat to Delancy—that scraggly-pelted, fox-faced, chicken-stealing excuse for an alpha."

Jace McKenna was Logan's closest friend and the alpha male of the Iron Tower pack. He had won the position with strength and wit when Logan's father had stepped down. Fortunately, Jace had plenty of intelligence and patience to go with his strength, but even he had his limits.

With a sigh, Logan ran his hand over his forehead, rubbing at the headache that had begun to form there. "You got the buck ready?"

"Yeah, we took it down last night. Made the same cubs who hunted on Twin Pines turf do the job, then took their kill. Cade had 'em chastened and frustrated, tails between their legs."

Logan could hear the amusement in Jace's voice. "They need to learn. Good of your beta to take on the job."

"Welfare of the pack is paramount. Cade knows that, just like every other adult. Cub education's all part of it." Jace paused. "Besides, Cade didn't want to miss out on all the fun."

Logan chuckled. "Have Cade escort the cubs responsible to Twin Pines' gathering site. The cubs present the buck with full apology and appropriate submission. Delancy will have to be satisfied with that."

Jace's voice took on a hard note. "See to it. I won't have my beta humbled either." There was a pause, then a spate of creative cursing crackled over the line. "Sorry, Logan. Delancy gets my back up."

"Same here, Jace. I'll deal with it."

"I don't envy you your job, my friend. Pack liaison, having to deal with all us stiff-necked alphas."

"Alphas deal or get their asses kicked," Logan replied with mock severity.

"Oooh, tough guy. Maybe it's time you and I go another round."

"Considering the shape we were in after the last time we faced off, how about I stand you a round at Morgan's instead? Bring Cade when he gets back from the grovel-fest."

Morgan's was the local watering hole and very popular with the local werewolf packs. It also carried the distinction of being a free zone, no disputes of any kind allowed. You parked your ego at the door or your ass got re-parked outside.

"Oh yeah, he'll need a drink by then," Jace agreed. "In a couple hours then, Logan. You stand the first, I'll stand the next."

"Deal." Logan prepared to hang up.

"And you didn't even have to kick my ass," Jace bantered. "Your skills are improving."

"Fuck off," Logan growled, ending the call to Jace's hoot of laughter.

Ten minutes later he hung up on yet another alpha. "Posturing prick," he muttered.

Having to end the discussion with the threat of ripping Delancy a new one, instead of being able to tactfully coerce his agreement, left a bad taste in Logan's mouth. Still, he thought with a satisfied smirk, Delancy had backed down quick enough. The job had *some* redeeming qualities.

Being the equal and more of any alpha in strength, cunning and intelligence, Logan had no desire to lead a pack. His nature was too independent, his inclinations too solitary to deal with the everyday running of a pack. A fortunate thing, considering that when his father stepped down he would have had to fight his best friend for leadership of Iron Tower pack. It was anyone's guess how a real contest between Logan and Jace would have ended.

His alpha qualities were what made him perfect for Pack Liaison. He was their troubleshooter, a man with the right amount of diplomatic ability and pure raw physical strength to keep peace between the sometimes volatile packs. In days gone by, disputes between packs had been decided by bloody combat, and still were in some cases. But in these more modern times, with the world becoming smaller and keeping a low profile becoming harder, different, less noteworthy tactics were employed. After all, unexplained deaths and injuries caused by teeth and claws were hard to hide. And, even though they had a network of doctors who were either lupines themselves or trusted humans, word got around, drawing unwanted attention.

Highly respected, sometimes feared, Logan did his job with cool confidence, averting bloodshed and overt hostilities. So why was the thought of telling one stubborn human woman that she was his mate causing him a twinge of unease?

Chapter Two

ॐ

As the bell over the door rang, signaling the arrival of another customer, Bryn glanced around the side of the bookshelf she was stocking and quickly ducked back. Her heart gave a little jump and her stomach began to pitch and roll.

Logan Sutherland, six-feet-four-inches of mouthwatering masculine perfection—every inch of it spelling trouble. He'd been a frequent visitor ever since the shop opened. For weeks she'd felt the unspoken weight of his interest until he'd finally declared himself by asking her out. When she'd politely claimed to be busy, keeping her panic under wraps had taken every bit of restraint she could muster.

Truth was, and she hated to admit it even to herself, she found him intriguing. Since her divorce she'd dated, but her choices were limited to men who held little chance of touching her heart. Logan was nowhere near that category and despite the attraction she felt, fear held the upper hand.

"Afternoon, Clare." His smooth deep voice rolled over Bryn, causing shivers to race up her spine. "I've come to pick up the latest Clancy you're holding for me."

"Sure thing, Logan." Clare's voice became muffled as she ducked under the counter to retrieve the book. "It's right here."

The bookstore was pristine, as usual. Shelves marched down the center of the store and lined both the sides and back. All neat, orderly and prominently labeled by subject. The lounging nooks were cozy and inviting. A few late customers browsed in various locations around the store. "Bryn around?" Logan inquired politely.

Mouthing a silent oath, Bryn's fist went to her mouth and she bit down. Hard.

Clare seemed to be trying to cover for her, but Bryn could tell she wasn't able to lie with Logan's clear, golden brown gaze fixed on her. "I…um."

Bryn wrinkled her nose in disgust at her friend's sudden inability to form a coherent sentence. "I'm right here," Bryn called out, coming to Clare's rescue. Marching up to the counter, she gave Clare a hard look.

Clare gave a helpless shrug. "I'll just go and—ah— check on something."

An amused smile tilted Logan's beautifully chiseled lips. Bryn gave an inward sigh of appreciation.

"I know why you're here." She decided to go on the offensive. "And the answer is no. I have appalling taste in men. If I say yes, it'll just turn out to be a big disaster for both of us, so I'm going to save us both a lot of trouble and embarrassment."

Logan struggled to keep his pleasant smile from turning into a full-fledged grin. *Lord, she's adorable*, he thought. Out loud he said, "Don't you think that's rather high-handed?"

"Why?" Bryn asked defensively.

"This decision affects both of us and I didn't get a vote," Logan replied, his tone mildly reproving.

Bryn stood nonplussed for a moment. "But it's *my* decision to make," she pointed out reasonably. Hoping to discourage Logan, she began inventing. "Besides, I discovered I'm a closet lesbian."

A strangled snort of laughter came from several shelves back. Logan's own amusement threatened to burst free. Keeping a strict rein on it, he uttered a bland, "Oh? Do you have a current lover?"

"Yes." Bryn cast about desperately for a name. "It's Clare."

A muffled "Hey!" of protest issued from behind the shelves.

"That must have come as something of a shock to Brian."

"He loves it," Bryn invented with wild abandon. "We have threesomes." Seeing Logan's raised eyebrows and look of disbelief, she began to wind down. "It's great. Really an eye-opening experience. You should…oh, hell. Where did I lose you?"

Logan considered her solemnly, a glint of amusement in his eyes. "If you'd have said, say, Susan Whitley was your lover, I might have believed you. But Clare just didn't wash. I'm sure she'd agree with me."

"She does." The crisp reply floated over the shelves.

Trying to turn the conversation, Bryn exclaimed, "Susan Whitley's a lesbian? I had no idea." Seeing her conversational gambit go flat, Bryn sighed in defeat. Her eyes met Logan's and her body began to tighten and burn with the intensity of the fire she saw kindled there. She bit her lip as an unshakable look of determination mingled with the flames.

Logan held out his hand. "Come with me."

Taking a step back, Bryn shook her head and pointed at the clock on the wall. "We still have an hour 'til closing." The pitch and roll of her stomach took on tidal wave proportions.

"I'm sure Clare wouldn't mind finishing out the hour and closing by herself." Logan indicated Clare's presence at Bryn's back.

"I wouldn't mind at all," Clare agreed pleasantly.

"Clare!" Bryn hissed.

"I owed you for that lesbian threesome stuff," Clare smirked, handing Bryn her purse.

"Come on, Bryn." Logan took Bryn's limp hand and led her unresisting form out of the bookstore and down the street to the coffee shop.

* * * * *

Bryn slid across the vinyl seat of the booth Logan indicated. The smell of coffee and freshly baked apple pie permeated the air. She regarded him silently, resting her hands on the smooth tabletop as he took a place opposite her. A waitress immediately rushed over to take their order, all the while surreptitiously giving Logan the once-over.

Humph, Bryn's lips gave a disgruntled twitch. *He probably gets this kind of thing all the time*, she thought, waving away the polite offer of service.

Sending the waitress for coffee, Logan's gaze settled on Bryn. "You're frowning," he observed.

"What?"

Her irritated reply caused a ripple of amusement to cross his features. He reached out and placed his forefinger between her brows. "Right here."

His unexpected touch, and the heat she felt from it, caused a shiver to slide down her spine.

"Don't." Bryn began to draw back.

With lightning speed Logan captured one of the hands she rested on the table. "Don't be afraid, Bryn. I would never hurt you."

Bryn's breath caught in her lungs as she was momentarily stunned by his words. How did he know she was afraid? Her stomach did another quivering roll. Fortunately the waitress returned with Logan's coffee, giving her a chance to rally. She forced a casual smile and made her hand lie still in his. "What makes you think I'm afraid of you, Logan?"

"Male intuition?" Logan quipped, before taking a sip of his coffee. He could hardly tell her the truth. Just as when he hunted prey, he could sense her unease, smell her fear.

"I don't believe I've ever heard of men having intuition," Bryn answered somewhat caustically.

"You think only women have that ability?" Logan asked. He examined the hand he held in his own. Her fingers were long and slender, the nails neat, short and unadorned. His other hand joined the first and he began to gently explore the contours of hers. He cupped one hand under hers while the fingers of his other slid sensuously over her palm.

As the tips of Logan's fingers glided over her palm, Bryn convulsively tightened her thighs. His easy caress felt like it connected right at her center. She felt the first stirring of need pinch her belly, causing moisture to form between her clenched thighs. Her nipples grew taut and an involuntary shiver slid the length of her spine. She gave a strangled gasp. "Stop that."

Logan looked up. His golden brown eyes captured gray eyes gone wide with apprehension and, yes, arousal. The rich, heady fragrance of her awakening passion inundated his senses. The hardened tips of her nipples pressed pertly against her light summer blouse and he almost groaned at the thought of suckling her. Her unwilling excitement caused a tingle in Logan's groin. He fought to keep his already stiffening cock under control. "You'll have dinner with me tomorrow."

Formed not as a question but a statement of fact, Bryn took exception. "No." She pulled at her captured hand. Was it her imagination or the play of sunlight through the windows that made his eyes seem to glow?

With a supreme effort of will, she held herself still as Logan tightened his hold on her hand and studied her intently. Well acquainted with her own reflection, she knew what he was seeing. Long, tawny blonde hair that hung almost to her waist, wide gray eyes, framed by slim, shaped eyebrows. Full lips, a straight nose and well-defined cheekbones. Classic features arranged on an oval face.

A sudden unbidden image filled her mind. Her hair tossing wildly on his pillows while her eyes filled with heat and need. Her lips parting, swollen from his kisses, moans and pleas torn from her throat as his body moved over her, touching her, filling her. Their bodies melding and writhing with the torrid heat they'd created together.

Bryn felt her cheeks heat under his regard, grateful that he couldn't read the thoughts generated by her runaway imagination. Still, he must have sensed something. Bryn bit her lip at the speculative gleam in his eyes.

"I'll pick you up at seven," he stated, his tone brooking no argument. Logan was not about to allow her to back away. Not this time. No more waiting, no more. His wolf demanded its mate.

"Are you always so domineering?" she demanded, irritation overshadowing her unease.

"Only when I see something I want," he returned flatly.

"You're beginning to seriously annoy me, Logan." Bryn felt like squirming under his intense regard but vowed not to give him the satisfaction of seeing her unnerved.

A slow teasing smile curved his lips. "Good. If you're annoyed you won't have time to be afraid."

Lord above, the visions that skated through her mind at the hard, determined look of him! Her churning imagination again took control. Images of a half-naked Logan in pirate garb, ready to pillage her trembling body overwhelmed her. She certainly could feel her timbers shivering, she thought irreverently.

Bryn felt a reluctant smile pull at her own lips. Her crazy pirate fantasy had loosened her taut nerves. "All right, just don't expect too much."

"I'll expect only as much as you want to give," Logan assured, his expression innocent of nefarious intent. Of course, he intended to help her want to give quite a lot. Not just for his own pleasure, it was his duty as her future mate.

She regarded him suspiciously. "Why do I get the feeling I shouldn't find those words comforting? Am I missing something here?"

"Are you this distrustful with everyone or just me?" Curiosity and some consternation prompted the question.

Bryn considered, watching Logan as he waited patiently. Sitting here with him she had discovered how much she really did want to get to know him. She was tired of her solitary loneliness, and she felt drawn to him in a way she'd never felt with anyone before. Longing filled her heart. "I'm sorry, Logan." She felt the slight sting of tears and turned her head to look out the window that fronted the coffee shop. "My ex-husband's exploits pretty much depleted my stock of trust. It's not you." She felt resentment stir again at what her ex-husband had cost her. And anger at herself for how easily the tears of self-pity formed. She hated being afraid. Hated being unable to give her trust. This was the legacy bequeathed to her for being foolish enough to love him.

Logan reached out, taking her chin in his hand, turning her back to face him. His golden brown eyes were filled with understanding, "It's okay, baby. Before too long you'll know without a doubt that you can trust me. I promise you, Bryn."

Hearing his gently spoken words, and the sincere conviction in them, brought a stirring of hope. "I hope so, Logan," she murmured.

Using words he hoped would lighten her mood, a teasing light filled his eyes as a smile quirked his lips. "It'll happen, sweetheart. Trust me."

A crooked smile and then a small chuckle broke from her parted lips. "If you say so." It would be so wonderful if he were speaking the truth. She hardly dared hope, and yet the lure of it was so beguiling she let herself imagine what a life shared with this man would be like.

"No arguments?" Logan's eyes widened in surprise. "On that note of progress, let me walk you to your car."

She pursed her lips and wrinkled her nose. "I'm not that bad, am I?" Bryn asked.

Logan quirked an eyebrow at her.

"Okay. I am," she admitted.

A shared and mutual grin united them.

Bryn bit her lip as she felt the first shy, happy stirring of hope.

They slid out of the booth and Bryn waited as he reached for his wallet to pay the tab. Taking her hand again, he led her out onto the sidewalk and back to the bookstore. Bryn smiled at the feel of her hand in his. She felt kind of like a kid again, holding hands with her boyfriend. Glancing at their reflection in the store windows they passed, she sobered. Logan was certainly no boy. Bryn herself was tall, five-foot-nine in her stocking feet. Logan's size made her feel almost petite. Quite a novel feeling for her. Though not overweight, she'd always felt she needed to lose a few pounds. One disastrous date had likened her figure to Marilyn Monroe's in *Some Like It Hot*, right before he'd tried to grab a handful of breast.

Despite the grab, she liked the comparison. There was no doubt that Marilyn Monroe was hot. Some men liked their women with lush, full curves. Apparently Logan was one of them.

She also liked Logan's forceful, take-charge attitude. His confidence shone like a beacon, drawing her to him.

And the way he so naturally—and at every opportunity— touched her, making her feel protected and desired. It was a feeling she found herself appreciating more and more.

Logan's eyes were drawn to the graceful movements of his mate. Thank god she didn't strive to be one of those rail-thin boy clones so many women tried to emulate, he thought with gratitude. Certain key body parts, he noted, swayed and jiggled with a subtle motion that had his libido revving its engine. The image of mounting that voluptuous, curvy body and being cushioned by that oh-so sweet and generous flesh set his blood surging through his veins and pooling in his groin, creating a noticeable bulge in his jeans.

Anticipation tightened his body, but he sobered as he remembered the bleak expression in her eyes and the shimmer of tears she had tried to hide. He had hidden the rage he'd felt at the man who should have taken care of her. He felt his insides pinch at the thought of her pain. He was determined to erase her fear and fill her with joy. His mate would be happy. He would accept nothing less.

They passed the bookstore, which was already closed and locked up, walking through the short alleyway that lay between it and the card shop next door. Her car was parked in the small lot behind the stores. Heat shimmered off the blacktop, baked by the midafternoon sun.

Bryn fished her keys out of her purse and unlocked the door. She turned to Logan to say goodbye, only to discover she'd lost his attention. Standing still and alert, his head slightly raised, Bryn could almost believe he was scenting the air.

Not knowing how accurate her guess was, she watched him, unaware that Logan had scented an unfamiliar male lupine. In nature, when the male of a species felt his right to the female of his choice was threatened, he responded by demonstrating his ownership. Logan's wolf made him very much a creature of instinct. Unaware of the effect the interloper was having on him, Bryn was also unaware that she was about to be claimed.

She looked around, surveying the lot and surrounding buildings, seeing nothing. "Logan, what...?" she began, and found herself hauled into his arms.

Caught off-guard, Bryn had no time to utter a protest as Logan's lips sealed over hers. Her initial start of surprise quickly turned to pleasure and then to growing arousal. She melted into the heat of his embrace, feeling her center go liquid with need as his burgeoning erection pressed insistently against her stomach. The moisture which had formed earlier was joined by reinforcements that dampened her panties.

Logan was as steady as a centuries-old oak in a tumultuous storm and she instinctively clung to him, afraid to let go. Her mind, what was left of it, whirled in circles formed of inflamed desire. Of its own volition, her body took control, offering itself willingly for Logan's exploration. All her doubts and fears were burned to ash by his masterful handling of her quivering flesh.

She was flooded with sensation. The feel of corded muscles under her hands, the hot, musky smell of aroused male and the iron-hard press of his erection as it strained against her belly drove her toward a beckoning orgasm. When his hand took possession of her breast, gently working the generous swell of flesh, her vagina clenched, demanding to be filled. Bryn moaned, pressing herself urgently against him.

Her head reverberated with the satisfied growl he gave as she leaned into him. Through the increasing friction and pressure between them, she felt his cock as it hardened against her body. Bryn shivered as Logan's other hand wandered down to cup the full curve of her buttock, pulling her tight against him, kneading the firm flesh of her bottom. His mouth opened over hers, his tongue seeking entrance. She granted it with a gasp, accepting the textured velvet of it as it stroked wantonly over hers.

Dizziness assailed her as he plundered her mouth, his tongue licking and tangling with hers. His taste was compelling, addicting. The pungent, sweet, musky aroma of her sex rose to perfume the air.

The feel of Logan's fingers as they found and rolled her distended nipple was electrifying. His groan of arousal sent a quiver of anticipation through Bryn. She undulated against him in mindless need.

Another groan issued from Logan's throat, this one tinged with regret as he fought to pull away from her. Bryn whimpered a protest as he slowly eased back, placing small lingering kisses on her swollen lips.

"Look at me, baby," Logan ordered softly. He wanted to howl at the necessary, but thankfully temporary, cessation of his claim. His cock was not a happy camper, taking on a life of its own, twitching with agitation at being roused only to be denied the prize.

Bryn's eyes opened. Slightly glazed, the irises had darkened to a stormy bluish- gray. Her accelerated breathing began to steady as she focused on Logan. A rosy flush pinked her cheeks as sanity returned.

"All right now?" he smiled, tenderly stroking the heated blush of her cheek.

"F-fine." She cleared her throat at the unsteady sound of her voice. "I'm fine." She looked shaky and disoriented, like a sleeper suddenly and rudely awakened.

Logan opened her car door and directed her inside. With some discomfort, he squatted down in the doorway. "Do you have a pen and something to write on?" he asked.

She fumbled in her purse for a pen and the small notebook she kept handy for shopping lists. Bryn struggled to clear her head as she watched Logan scribble something on the pad, noting absently that he was left-handed. She also noted with more clarity the hard bulge in his jeans that had so recently prodded her. Her moist and yearning pussy again protested the absence of what it wanted. Especially when what it wanted was so…right there.

His firm, masculine erection called to her. *Look at me, touch me.* She imagined if it were exposed, that little eye at the tip would be winking with lascivious invitation. Her teeth sank into her lower lip again, this time with agitation. Disconcerted by her fall into outlandish fantasy, she quickly returned her gaze to his hands. The damage, however, was done. The combination of recent tactile sensation and the visual confirmation of his stellar attributes had her fighting not to squirm in her seat.

Aware of her perusal, proud to show her the effect she had on him and pleased to know she was just as affected, Logan handed the pen and pad back. "That's my cell phone. Call me when you get home."

"Why?" she inquired a bit acidly.

"I want to know you've gotten home safe," Logan replied, and seeing the light of battle in her eyes he leaned in and pressed a firm kiss to her lips. His own frustration level high, he was determined to have his way in this, if nothing else. "No arguments, Bryn. Call."

Still shaken by the passion that had risen so easily at his touch, Bryn decided a strategic retreat was in order. "All right, I'll call," she promised sulkily.

"Drive carefully, sweet." Logan ran a caressing finger down her cheek and stood. Closing her door, he stepped back and watched as she drove out of the lot, made a left turn and disappeared down the street.

Logan released a sigh of regret. Logically he knew he had done the right thing, letting her go. There was still the pending explanation of his background to be made, not to mention her unknowing role as his mate. Her arousal would have allowed him to go further, but when calmer heads prevailed he knew her trust would be a loss he'd not recover.

His smile was somewhat pained as he recalled the expression on her face. If she ached for him as much as he did for her, they were both in for a restless night. He let his eyes wander the area again. The fading scent of the lupine male drifted on the breeze. Despite the frustration of having to call a halt to what could have been an even more enjoyable activity, satisfaction filled his being. His claiming of Bryn had begun, and judging by her reaction she was more than receptive to him. Let this unknown witness testify to the fact that Bryn belonged to him.

* * * * *

Reece Cofield sauntered down the street to his waiting car. He anticipated the coming confrontation. Lillian was going to be one PO'd lupine when she heard his news. Logan Sutherland had chosen a mate.

He'd made no announcement and it was clear his formal claiming had yet to be made, but his intent was blatantly obvious, judging by his actions in the parking lot a few moments ago. Reece knew Logan had caught his scent. There was no mistaking Logan's marking of his territory.

The girl he'd been with was a pretty one for sure. Reece, had he not already committed himself to Lillian, wouldn't have minded a piece of that himself. Of course, having to go through Logan put a halt to those pleasant thoughts. He might be horny, but he certainly wasn't stupid. Getting behind the wheel of his car, he grinned as he headed to Lillian's place. She was going to be furious. Lillian had the crazy notion that she was going to make Logan her pet. Granted, they'd had one sexual encounter several years ago, but Logan had made it more than clear that he had no interest in a permanent pairing.

Maybe now Lillian would take Reece's own pairing urges more seriously. If nothing else, he knew he was in for a hell of a ride tonight. Once Lillian got over her rage and calmed down she'd be primed for action. He drove away, feeling his cock quiver and thicken in anticipation.

Chapter Three

෨

Bryn drove home in something of a daze. Luckily, there was very little traffic in the small town of Whispering Springs at this time of day. She reached her destination and pulled into a driveway shaded by a huge oak tree. Leaving the car parked in front of the garage, she made her way up the steps of the little house she'd bought when she first moved to town.

Unlocking the front door, Bryn stepped inside the familiar haven of home and gave an enormous sigh of relief. She automatically kicked off her shoes and dropped her purse and keys on the side table, stopping to gaze at her reflection in the mirror that hung above it.

I look stunned, she thought. Bryn noted her slightly swollen, kiss-stung lips and slowly ran her tongue over them as she brought back the feel of Logan's lips on hers. His taste clung to her mouth and she savored the dark, haunting flavor of him. She'd never been so quickly and easily aroused in any man's arms. A wicked little smile curved her lips as she felt the sticky warmth of her body's juices as it had prepared to receive Logan's. She felt the slow tingle of desire begin to burn higher. He sure knew how to kiss. Bryn was sure Logan knew how to do a lot of other interesting things, as well.

She wandered into the living room. Her furnishings were an eclectic mix of styles, chosen for comfort and the subtle way they complimented each other. The colors were warm and natural, beige, brown and gold with a vibrant splash of orange in the form of several throw rugs. The decor encouraged ease and informality. She snatched up the phone before stretching out on the sofa. Closing her eyes, she replayed the feeling of being in Logan's arms. His body was so warm and hard, and the way he held her? Exhilarating seemed too tame a word to describe it. He'd surrounded her, controlled her, all the while ensuring her pleasure. Bryn felt her body begin to thrum at the thought of his erection, which had pressed so boldly against her belly. The hard length of it had been quite impressive. The vibrator waiting upstairs was running a poor second in comparison, the thought of using it unappealing. With a dissatisfied grimace she took up the phone and punched in the numbers Logan had given her.

As the phone rang, Bryn felt a quiver of anticipation. Her hand slid deliberately up her thigh, the material of her skirt rising. He picked up on the second ring. With just a hello, the deep, rich timbre of his voice sent a shaft of need straight to her already wet core. Bryn closed her eyes and stifled a moan as her swelling sex blossomed like a flower under the coaxing rays of the sun.

"It's Bryn, Logan," she managed, hoping her voice didn't sound as breathless as she felt.

"Hi, baby, I take it you made it home okay?" Logan's voice flowed over Bryn's senses, inundating her with desire.

Seemingly of its own volition, her wandering hand glided between her thighs and a slender finger slithered under the damp crotch of her panties and into the slick channel of her soaked pussy.

"Oh yeah. No problems." Bryn bit her lip as her finger slid through the thick syrup, spreading it up, over and around the taut bud of her clit. A naughty thrill shot up her spine as she arched in reaction.

"If it's all right with you, I thought we'd go to O'Neal's," Logan offered. "I'm in the mood for one of their steaks."

"That sounds good," she managed. The rocketing rise of her need tightened her throat, making it almost impossible to speak. Her voice came out a husky rasp.

There was a pause on the other end of the phone line. "Bryn, baby, what are you doing?" Logan's voice had deepened, drifting silkily over her body.

Bryn froze. "Nothing."

He knew. Somehow he knew. She wasn't sure whether to melt with humiliation or stimulation.

"I know I got you stirred up in the parking lot. You're touching yourself, aren't you? Are you wet, sweetheart?" His voice was lazy and hot.

"Logan, that's obscene!" Caught, Bryn wasn't yet ready to confess to him. She wanted desperately to deny the need coursing through her body. She couldn't. The smooth pad of her finger settled over her clit, gently manipulating the sensitized nub.

"There's nothing obscene about it, Bryn. The truly obscene thing would be to deny your needs, to deny your pleasure. I can be there in fifteen minutes, baby," he cajoled. "There's nothing I want more than to see to your pleasure."

Indecision rioted side by side with a pending hormonal meltdown. "Logan, I...I'm not ready for that," Bryn panted.

"Then let me help you this way, honey, right now." A heated thread of arousal wound through the deep calm of his voice. "Are your panties off?"

Bryn felt her vagina clench at his boldness. "Oh god...no," she admitted. Her breath and heart rate began to accelerate.

"Take them off for me, baby," Logan coaxed. "In my mind I'm seeing you lying there with your thighs spread wide and your sweet wet pussy exposed to me. You have beautiful long fingers, Bryn. I can see them sinking into your tight pussy as you fuck yourself."

"I don't think I can do this." Bryn was stunned by how quickly her need had grown. Her sex felt open, yearning to be filled. Sharing this with Logan made her feel wild, and yet she was afraid to expose so much of herself to him. Afraid of what he would think of her.

"Yes you can, sweet. We'll pleasure each other. Just close your eyes and listen to the sound of my voice. Now take off those panties, baby."

The hot sensual growl of his voice galvanized her into action. Lifting her hips, Bryn slid her panties down her legs and over her feet, dropping them on the floor. She spread her thighs wide and sank her fingers into her ready channel. A breathy moan left her parted lips and winged its way over the phone line to Logan. His answering groan of satisfaction came back to her.

"That's right, sweetheart. It feels so good, doesn't it, baby? I'm right there with you." The hot sensual whisper of Logan's voice flowed over Bryn. "Our fingers are buried deep in your pussy. Bring our fingers up and glide them over your clit, Bryn."

Bryn was defenseless against her raging need and Logan's heated dictates. She obeyed and cried out at the stunning pulse of pleasure that contracted her creaming channel. "Logan, oh god, Logan!" she chanted distractedly.

"Are you that close, Bryn? Damn, baby, you're killing me. Listen to me, Bryn. I'm stroking my cock. It's big and thick and long and ready to burst just for you. I'm touching you and you're touching me. Our fingers are wrapped tight around my shaft and we're squeezing and pumping. I'm going to come in your hands."

The sudden visual of Logan, buck naked with a massive hard-on, caused another gush of thick cloying liquid to coat Bryn's probing fingers.

"Logan, are you really stroking your cock?" Her voice was tight, quivering with excitement.

"Oh yeah, babe. Do you like that, Bryn? Would you like to watch me sometime, sweetheart?"

Bryn groaned, her pussy clenching and creaming at the thought of watching Logan masturbate. "Yesss," she hissed. "Would you do that for me? Let me watch you?"

"You know I would, Bryn. Whatever you need, baby, whatever you want. Slip your fingers back inside that tight, creamy pussy. Those are *my* fingers, Bryn. Soon it will be my cock inside you. I'm between your thighs, Bryn. We're going to fuck now, baby. *Now.*"

Bryn continued to fuck her fingers in and out of her juicy passage, then slid them over the hard nub of her clit again and again. Her hips undulated mindlessly as whimpers and breathless moans burned over the phone line.

"Are you ready to come, Bryn? Let me hear you, baby. Come for me."

She pictured Logan vigorously stroking the thick, hard length of his cock. She could hear the panting of his breath. Her desperate rise to climax became his as they labored together. The physical and mental inundation, combined with the graphic sensual tone of his voice as he coaxed her, sent Bryn plunging over the edge.

* * * * *

Logan hadn't anticipated Bryn's physical state when she called. Knowing that he had aroused her to the point that she was willing to indulge in self-pleasuring over the phone, with his encouragement, was enough to make him howl. Her husky, panting breaths were sending tingles of pure lust straight to his straining cock.

One-handed, he held the phone, deftly unbuttoning his shirt. He released the button at the top of his jeans and carefully slid the zipper down over a cock that quivered to be set free. He pulled his shirttail loose and released his full, aching erection. With a sigh, he settled himself on the sofa. His groin tightened with anticipation as her soft moans ghosted over the phone line.

Logan lay entranced, instructing and cajoling her, listening to her breathless reactions as she touched the body he knew would soon be his. All the while, he stroked his turgid cock, imagining her hands and mouth working him, pleasuring him. The pressure built, he ached to come, but waited, waited for her. Finally, a hairsbreadth from release, her wailing cry broke Logan's control, and his own strangled shout of pleasure joined hers.

He shot stream after stream of thick creamy cum over his hand and onto the rock- hard stomach exposed by his open shirt and jeans. Hearing a long drawn-out "Mmmm" of pleasure, he smiled lazily. Her sighs of satisfaction enhanced his own pleasure. Unadulterated joy filled his being. His mate was not only beautiful, but filled with a fire that could burn a man to ash. Life had never tasted so sweet.

Silence reigned, but for the panting of two people recovering from nirvana.

Bryn moaned softly as multiple aftershocks quivered through her. She rode the decreasing ripples as they gently lowered her back to reality. As her head cleared, Bryn began to feel shocked at what she had just done. How could she have been so brazen? She'd just engaged in a red-hot bout of phone sex with a man she hadn't even dated yet. What must he be thinking? That she did this with just anyone? She'd lost him before they'd even had a chance. She turned to lie on her side and spoke quietly into the receiver. "You must think I'm quite the slut."

A momentary silence greeted her declaration as she waited for his condemnation. Tears filled her eyes.

"If you ever say that again, I'll paddle your sweet ass so hard you won't be able to sit for a week." Logan's voice was stern as he issued the reprimand. "Is that clear?"

Bryn felt her throat close as tears misted her wide gray eyes.

"Answer me, Bryn," he ordered.

"Yes, it's clear."

There was a momentary pause before Logan spoke. "What I *think*, sweetheart, is that you are a warm, sensuous woman who just shared a beautiful, exciting and downright mind-blowing experience with me. I'm humbled by your gift, Bryn."

"Logan," she whispered, struggling to maintain her composure and not turn into a weeping puddle of sentimental ooze. "That's the sweetest thing anyone's ever said to me."

"You're not going to cry are you, baby?" His soothing tone washed over her. "Tell me you're all right or I'm coming over there right now. I don't want you upset."

Bryn could hear the caring and concern in Logan's voice and it made her smile. "I'm okay. You don't need to come charging over here."

"Are you sure?"

"Yes."

"Really sure?"

Bryn gave a brief laugh. Logan's worry filled her with warmth of a different kind than that they had just shared. "Yes, I'm *really* sure."

"I'll pick you up tomorrow at seven then, Bryn. Sleep well tonight, baby. Dream of me."

"Is that an order?" she teased.

"A strong suggestion," Logan rejoined.

"In that case I'll give it some thought," she conceded. "Goodnight, Logan."

With Logan's "goodnight, sweetheart" bringing a smile to her lips, Bryn hit the talk button on the phone, cutting the connection. Logan had been so sweet and understanding. And so commanding. She hugged tight the happiness that surged through her. She'd subconsciously longed for a man who would have the confidence and strength of character to dominate her, not with cruelty, but with love and caring. And all those endearments, she thought. *Sweetheart, baby, honey.* "I like it," she murmured, and stretched luxuriously on the sofa. Rising, she picked up her discarded panties and headed to the bathroom for a nice hot shower.

On the way, revelation struck.

"I came without a vibrator. Yes!"

Chapter Four

ഇ

Ready promptly at seven, Bryn waited nervously for Logan's arrival. Dressed for the warm August weather, she wore a dress of peach-colored gauze that fell to mid-calf. It had short sleeves, a deep, scooped neckline and delicate embroidery on the bodice. The full skirt fluttered delicately in the breeze. Sandals with peach-colored straps adorned her slim feet and she'd painted her finger and toenails to match. She'd had a wonderful night's sleep, and in fact, had had a very nice — if somewhat confusing — dream about Logan. Something to do with a sultry moonlit night and a walk in the forest, which culminated in a passionate interlude at the side of a cool stream.

Everything in the dream had seemed so sharp and clear, except Logan and herself. She knew it was him, could feel him and taste him but she couldn't see him. Except for his eyes. Golden, amber eyes that glowed with an otherworldly luminescence. Eyes that should have been frightening but were strangely compelling.

Bryn put those thoughts away as Logan's car pulled into the drive. Her insides clenched. She'd hoped she would get over the fluttering stomach that attacked every time she saw him. Apparently it wasn't going to happen tonight.

He gracefully exited the car and walked to the porch where she waited in dazed silence. "Oh my god," she breathed. The reality of the situation rolled over her like an avalanche. "I'm going out with a studmuffin."

Logan walked with the smooth, sure glide of a predator certain of its mastery. He was dressed simply in black and white. Black boots, tight black jeans and a loose white shirt opened at the neck to reveal the beginning of the crisp dark curls that she knew must cover the expanse of his hard-muscled chest.

The setting sun shimmered in his sable hair, displaying flowing glints of gold and red. He reached up and removed the sunglasses that shaded his eyes and brought them to bear on her unmoving form, enfolding her in the golden warmth of his gaze.

A shiver of recognition passed over her—the fundamental recognition of the female when she acknowledges the presence of an alpha male. Alpha males required submission. Needs she'd never fully acknowledged or explored came to the fore. Visions of being dominated, all control taken away, caused roils of agitation and confusion.

Bryn was consumed with conflicting emotions, from pure primal lust to a fear that prompted her need for self-preservation. To put herself in this man's power, to give him her trust, was the most tempting and terrifying thing she had ever faced.

She forced herself to remain still, though she felt the urge to turn and run, locking herself in and him out. She bravely met his admiring gaze.

Logan approached the porch and studied Bryn. She looked sweet and innocent in her gauzy peach-colored dress. Her tawny blonde hair shone and the color of her dress accented the light golden tint of her smooth, warm skin. A silent growl rumbled though Logan's chest. He knew the passion that hid under that guileless exterior. The big, bad wolf was eager to play. To the casual observer she seemed cool and composed, but Logan could sense the turmoil within. His highly acute vision detected the dilation of her pupils and the darkening of the surrounding iris as her emotions whirled. He could smell the beginnings of her arousal as well as the fear that tainted it.

The instinctive need to take the female of his choice rode him hard. Had she been any other woman he would let his dominant nature rule and take what he wanted. His past partners had been savvy to his needs and expectations and knew that theirs was but a temporary arrangement. There was no need for caution or stealth. Mutual hungers were fed, both partners were satisfied, and the relationship ended without anger or recrimination.

Bryn was unexpected. That she was his mate was indisputable, and his right to take her undeniable, but in spite of her sometimes tough and prickly exterior, she was possessed of a tender heart and a gentle soul. And she had been hurt. Her trust betrayed, her confidence undermined.

The wolf knew of her need to be dominated and controlled. The man knew of her need for tenderness and reassurance. To push too hard in any direction would bring failure. Together, his dual nature sought a balance that would bring them the reward of Bryn's trust and love.

Logan climbed the steps to the porch, his eyes steady and unwavering, he came to a halt in front of her. "You look beautiful, sweetheart."

"Thank you," she replied shyly, sincerely pleased at his words of praise.

"Now relax. There are no earthshaking decisions to be made. Nothing bad is going to happen. We're going to get to know each other a little better and hopefully enjoy each other's company. Okay?"

Bryn nodded and felt herself relax just a fraction, until his hand came up to cup her chin and his mouth descended and settled over hers. Her tension level went sky-high, leveled out and collapsed as she melted into the warmth of his tender kiss. His lips moved slowly over hers, rubbing and sliding until they found the perfect fit. Bryn's lips parted on a sigh and Logan's tongue glided in with languorous ease, slowly exploring the heated cavern of her mouth. His tongue grazed hers, petting and encouraging her participation. Bryn willingly complied and followed his tongue back into his mouth to begin her own slow, sultry explorations.

Logan growled his approval and reluctantly pulled back, ending the kiss. "Unless you want the evening to end right now — with me taking you here on the porch — I suggest we get going," he warned, his words tempered by a teasing smile.

Bryn blushed as the memory of last night's phone sex session crossed her mind. "Let's go," she insisted. Knowing all too well how easily Logan roused her desire, she grabbed his hand and pulled him across the porch and down the steps.

"By the way, I forgot to thank you," he said with a twitch of his lips.

"For what?" Bryn asked as Logan seated her in the passenger seat. She watched as he rounded the car and eased into the driver's seat.

"For what?" she questioned again, frowning in puzzlement.

Logan started the car and backed out the driveway. "I don't believe I've ever been called a studmuffin before."

Stunned silence filled the car, then Bryn began to sputter. "How did you...you couldn't have heard...Logan!"

Masculine laughter filled the car as it accelerated and glided smoothly down the street.

* * * * *

Several hours later the remnants of their meal was cleared away and Bryn gave Logan a considering look. He'd been such a change from her usual dates. His manners were without fault, he was polite and considerate of her as well as the waitstaff. His sense of humor was sharp and delightful. He spoke with intelligence and wit on a variety of subjects. His inquisitive nature drew her as they explored each other with carefully worded inquiries.

And through it all, he sparked a level of excitement within her that she was hard-pressed to keep in check. The heated look in his eyes drifted over her skin like ghostly fingers until she felt scorched. Anticipation simmered and all trepidation seemed to disappear as she contemplated the possibilities.

O'Neal's had been the perfect choice for their first date. The booths were high-backed and cozy, giving the diners the illusion of privacy. The decor was elegant, but not glacial. As to dress, one could be as formal or relaxed as one wished. And the food was out of this world excellent. But what really put it over the top in Bryn's book was its familiarity. In this situation, with Logan's presence so exciting and nerve-racking, familiar surroundings helped keep her calm.

Their waitress stopped by to refill their glasses of iced tea, causing a pause in the conversation. Bryn rested her chin in her hand and studied Logan thoughtfully.

"What deep, dark thought is roaming through your head, sweet?" Logan inquired, smiling.

"Why do I get the feeling that sometimes you can read my mind?" Bryn asked with perfect seriousness, whimsically wondering if he could picture the thoughts forming in her head. "You can't, can you?"

Logan scoffed. "Hardly."

He reached out and gently grazed his fingers down the silken skin of her cheek. "You have very expressive eyes. And I've always been adept at reading body language."

"Oh?" Bryn was intrigued. "What does my body language tell you?"

Logan became serious as he considered her. "You're relaxing, your movements are natural, not tense or studied. Your eyes meet mine directly, without embarrassment, and with a certain amount of speculation. Your conversation is smooth, not stilted. You're opening yourself up to me, revealing yourself.

"I'd say you're losing your fear of what's developing between us. You're enjoying my company. You're happy. And by the slight darkening of your eyes every now and then, I'd say you're wondering what it will be like when we make love."

Bryn listened in amazed silence. It felt like he was looking into her soul. It seemed astounding that such an open and easy connection had formed between them so quickly. She felt a blush heat her cheeks and a frisson of nerves tighten her chest as his last remark hit home with such accuracy.

"So how close am I?" His gaze, although teasing, demanded the truth.

"Close, really close," Bryn admitted bravely.

"I intend to get closer, Bryn," Logan vowed. The sultry heat in his voice caressed her.

"Logan, I..." she began, then halted as Logan's attention was diverted by the approach of a man and woman. Bryn noted the flare of his nostrils and the wary glint in his eyes. The couple were strangers to her, but apparently known to Logan. She watched him as he rose to his feet, his stance clearly aggressive.

"Logan, you're looking as handsome as ever." The woman who spoke leaned in, placing a kiss on his cheek.

"Lillian." His expression remained neutral as he turned to the man who accompanied her. "I don't believe I've met your friend, although he does seem familiar."

Logan's words held a subtle challenge. Bryn glanced at him, puzzled by his attitude.

The man held out his hand. "Reece Cofield," he introduced himself. "And you're right, we've never been *formally* introduced."

Bryn examined the couple curiously.

The woman was tall and dark with exotic features, her medium-length hair a smooth, stylish wave. She wore a short, slinky, black dress that sported a flirty fringe at the hem, which ended mid-thigh, revealing shapely legs. The three-inch heels of her—as Bryn thought of them—slut shoes, added to the overall picture of sex on the hoof.

The man was her equal in height and wholesomely handsome, with sandy blond hair and blue eyes. Bryn found his somewhat deferential behavior toward Logan curious.

Taking possession of Logan's arm, Lillian turned her attention to Bryn. "Introduce me to your companion, Logan," she ordered playfully.

"Bryn Roydan, meet Lillian Adair and her friend, Reece Cofield."

"Aren't you just the sweetest thing," Lillian declared in a sugary tone dripping with venom. "I just love that dress, dear. You're so fortunate to be able to pull off the 'schoolmarm' look."

Instead of being angry, amusement bubbled inside Bryn as she raised an eyebrow at Lillian's backhanded compliment. "Why, thank you," Bryn returned. "I envy you, though. Your outfit is stunning. Anyone without your class and sophistication would look like just another high-class hooker."

Two strangled snorts of male amusement brought a glare from Lillian, who regrouped and headed in another direction. She was determined to take this puny human down a peg. Her hand caressed Logan's arm. "I've missed you, Logan. I look forward to our next night together."

A swirl of conflicting emotions emanated from the four, suddenly thrown into a frozen tableau.

Bryn's reaction, a prompt twinge of hurt, was quickly hidden. A quick glance in his direction revealed Logan's fast-fading amusement being replaced by anger and disgust. Logan's past was his own business, she realized. Still, confronted with the knowledge that he had had a relationship with this beautiful, if totally bitchy, female was a blow. She avoided the glance he sent in her direction.

Instead she redirected her attention to Lillian and was somewhat surprised to see a flash of regret in her eyes as she gazed at Reece. To Bryn, Lillian's reaction seemed to reveal her feelings for the man. So why humiliate him this way?

Chagrin and disappointment seemed to radiate from Reece. Anger simmered in his eyes as he neatly peeled Lillian away from Logan.

"Come on, Lillian," he urged, breaking the frozen silence. "I'm sure Bryn and Logan have better things to do than stand around chitchatting."

Turning at Reece's urging, Lillian dropped her purse, spilling the contents. She uttered a cry of dismay. "Oh dear, how clumsy of me!"

Logan and Reece bent to retrieve her scattered belongings, each anxious, for different reasons, to help Lillian on her way. "Bryn, dear, there's a lipstick right by your foot if you'd be so kind," she pointed out sweetly.

Before so artfully dumping her purse, Lillian had palmed a small vial of liquid in her hand. With everyone's attention diverted, no one noticed as she poured it with surreptitious haste into Bryn's waiting glass. Her expression held smug amusement before she cleared it.

With her possessions restored, Lillian took Reece's arm, thanking them for their help. "Have a wonderful evening," she trilled. Her knowing smirk was hidden as she turned and led Reece away.

Logan resumed his seat and met Bryn's expectant look. "One night, two years ago," he stated, agitation making him run a restless hand through his hair. "Hell, not even the night. I knew it was a mistake as soon as it happened."

"You apparently made a big impression on her," Bryn pointed out, unknowingly sipping her doctored tea.

Logan grimaced. "Lillian's not impressionable. She collects men. It intrigues her when someone turns her down. It's the 'wanting the unattainable' syndrome. If I'd fawned all over her she'd have thrown me over." He paused thoughtfully. "If Cofield wants her to take him seriously, he'd better start showing a little backbone. Lillian doesn't respond to kindness, she's too much the dominating bitch. She needs someone whose strength equals her own."

Bryn's eyebrows rose at Logan's in-depth analysis of Lillian. "You seem to know her pretty well for someone you only spent a few hours with." Her voice dripped with sarcasm.

Logan grinned, unperturbed by Bryn's waspish observation and secretly enjoying his mate's possessive behavior. "I'm also a very observant student of human nature, baby."

Her "hmmm" was filled with dubiousness, but she dropped the subject. Logan's voice rang with sincerity and his eyes held unquestionable truth. She leaned forward, pinning him with her gaze. "Logan, what do you do?"

"Do?" *Here we go*, he thought. This was going to be tricky.

"You know, for a living. I've never heard you or anyone else mention what kind of work you do."

Logan mentally crossed his fingers. "I guess you could say I'm self-employed."

"As what?" Bryn inquired.

"As a sort of consultant," Logan embroidered, pleased to be skating somewhat close to the truth.

Bryn continued to probe. "Whom do you consult with and about what?"

Logan knew he couldn't dodge her questions with vague generalities for long. "As to the what, I consult on many topics, I'm sort of a glorified troubleshooter. And the whom? That's going to have to remain confidential for now."

Bryn's brows drew together and she gave him a sort of frowning smile. "You interest me, Logan. You're not a spy are you?"

Logan laughed and denied the accusation. "I'll tell you in time, honey," he promised, "but first you and I are going to have to have a very serious discussion." Forestalling any new questions, Logan rose, reaching for his wallet to pay the waiting check. "Are you ready to go?"

"I am," she conceded, allowing him his less-than-satisfactory explanation. She followed Logan's example and rose from her seat. While he counted out bills to pay the check she reached for her iced tea and downed the rest of the contents of the icy glass.

The night air had cooled somewhat and Bryn welcomed the warmth of the arm Logan draped over her shoulders as they exited the restaurant. Walking to the car, she felt a sudden swirl of dizziness. She grasped Logan's arm, holding on until the spinning stopped.

"What is it, baby? Are you all right?" Logan's concerned face swam into focus.

"I felt a little dizzy there for a minute. I hope I'm not coming down with something," she commented, disgusted at the thought. "I hate to be sick."

"If you get sick, we'll play doctor until you're all better," Logan teased with an exaggerated leer that had Bryn laughing.

Logan opened the car door and Bryn carefully settled herself inside. Something was definitely wrong. Her movements felt halting and unsure. Her hands shook as her coordination began to deteriorate. She was having trouble with the seat belt and as Logan leaned near to help, her wide eyes met his with growing distress.

"Hold on, sweetheart, I'll get you home," he soothed quietly.

Bryn nodded as Logan closed her door and rounded the car. A tremor shook her body as a strong cramp gripped her stomach. She swallowed hard, mortified at the thought of throwing up in Logan's beautiful car.

"Hurry, Logan," she pleaded. "I'm really starting to feel sick."

"Try and relax, Bryn. Put your head back and close your eyes, we'll be there soon." He strove to keep his voice calm, his worry hidden.

Logan drove with quick efficiency, the lateness and absence of traffic easing their way. Slowing only long enough to determine the way was clear, he passed through red lights and stop signs.

Bryn broke out in a cold sweat, and soft moans unconsciously passed her lips as she fought to maintain control. She was oblivious to her surroundings.

Unbeknownst to her, her sudden illness had raised Logan's suspicions. He pulled out his cell phone and made a call.

The car slowed and pulled into a long, winding drive. Bryn opened her eyes and fought to focus. "This isn't my house," she murmured, as the partial brick and stone façade swam into view.

"No, it's mine. It was closer, sweetheart, and Dr. Maigrey's on his way."

Disoriented and fighting her stomach's imminent eruption, Bryn made no protest as Logan gently gathered her in his arms and carried her into the house. The weightless, swaying motion she experienced as he carried her was almost her undoing.

"Bathroom, hurry," she croaked.

She held on tight as he took the stairs two at a time, depositing her in the bathroom just in time. Bryn went to her knees in front of the toilet and lost her struggle. Several minutes later she realized that Logan was still with her.

"God, Logan, get out of here," she gasped as another cramp hit.

"Not a chance. Just let it go, baby. I'm staying right here."

Bryn felt his arm encircle her middle, his hand splayed on her midriff, lightly rubbing. His other hand held back her hair. He crooned soft, comforting words as she fought her way through each spasm.

When her paroxysms finally slowed, Logan grabbed a washcloth, soaking it with cool water. Bryn closed her eyes as he ran it carefully over her face. Her eyelids and lips were slightly swollen, her complexion waxen pale. When she opened her eyes he smiled sympathetically.

"This has got to be the most humiliating experience of my life," Bryn revealed. She was exhausted, her thoughts muddled.

"Logan!" a strong male voice hailed from downstairs.

"Dr. Maigrey," Logan explained, squeezing her shoulder. He walked into the bedroom to yell down, "Up here, doc."

Dr. John Maigrey entered the bathroom with an air of calm confidence. "What seems to be the trouble here?" he asked, and listened as Logan explained. He watched Bryn, observing the pale clammy skin, dilated pupils and unsteady movements. As he leaned in to listen to her heart with his stethoscope, he caught a faint, but familiar odor.

"Have you taken any prescription or over-the-counter meds in the last few hours, Bryn?" At her negative response he prepared a syringe. "I'm going to take a small blood sample," he explained.

Eyeing the needle, she felt her stomach tighten again. "Go away for a minute, please?" she pleaded.

"Young lady, I've seen just about everything the human body can excrete. You go right ahead and do what you need to do."

Helplessly, Bryn turned and greeted what appeared to be her new best friend. Afterward Logan again wiped her face. "This is turning into a real red letter day for me," she quipped in spite of her discomfort. "I've now thrown up in front of two handsome men instead of just one." Slow tears of helpless frustration trickled down her pale cheeks.

"It's all right, baby," Logan soothed, gathering her close and slowly rocking her as he rubbed her back.

"Don't rock, Logan," Bryn begged, as she struggled to get herself under control. "It's like being on a boat. I get seasick, too," she warned, as Logan urged her to sit on the rim of the tub.

Dr. Maigrey smiled at her comment as he took the blood sample, then filled another syringe with a small amount of fluid from a little bottle. "I'm going to give you a shot that should stop the nausea," he explained.

"Bless you," she breathed sincerely, wincing only slightly at the pinch of the needle. Relief loosened her tense muscles.

"That should do it, dear. I want you to rest. Drink plenty of fluids as soon as your stomach settles. You need to recoup some of your losses," he ordered kindly.

"Thank you, Dr. Maigrey," Bryn replied, her gratitude plainly apparent. "I really appreciate you helping me. I didn't think doctors made house calls anymore."

"Well, Logan and I go back a few years and I owe him a favor or two. You take care of yourself, Bryn. I'll let you know the results of the blood test." He surreptitiously motioned for Logan to follow him out of the bathroom.

"I need to talk to you," John explained softly as he headed toward the bedroom door.

"Let me get Bryn settled and I'll be right down," Logan agreed. "Help yourself to a drink or raid the kitchen if you like."

He smoothed the frown from his face and returned to the bathroom to find Bryn still perched on the edge of the tub. He knelt in front of her, smoothing back her hair. "Feel better, sweetheart?"

She nodded tiredly. "Yeah." Her eyes looked huge in her pale face, and were accentuated by the dark circles that had formed under them. She reached out with trembling fingers and softly brushed the warm skin of his cheek. "Thank you."

Logan felt touched to his very soul at the depth of meaning conveyed by her eyes, the gesture, and her simple words. He engulfed her cold hands in his, transferring his warmth to her. "I'll always take care of you, Bryn," he promised.

She smiled. "Are you going to take me home now?"

"No, baby, you're staying here where I can keep an eye on you. And you may as well save yourself the trouble of arguing. It's non-negotiable," Logan warned her with gentle determination.

She considered her options and gave in without a fight. "Okay. Do you have a toothbrush I can use?"

Logan grinned and chucked her playfully under the chin. "Smart girl." He chuckled as she stuck her tongue out at him. He supplied her with the toothbrush and disappeared into the bedroom, reappearing with a t-shirt and the robe his mother had given him one Christmas that he rarely wore.

"Thought you could use these," he explained, laying them on the counter by the sink. "Do you want to take a bath or shower before bed?" At her nod he pulled a couple of clean towels out of the cupboard. "You should take a bath," he suggested. "You might get dizzy standing under the shower. Or," he paused, trying to look innocent but failing utterly as a wicked smile graced his lips, "you could wait for me and I'll shower with you. Just to make sure you don't fall," he qualified.

Bryn frowned. "You've already had the privilege of seeing me barf," she intoned sarcastically. "There are only so many intimacies I'm allowing in one day. Get out."

Logan felt relief at her ability to banter. She was feeling better.

"I'll go," he conceded, placing a kiss on her forehead. "But be careful."

As the door closed behind him, Bryn sank to the tub's rim, her knees unsteady. Gathering her waning strength, she brushed her teeth and slowly undressed. Adjusting the water temperature, she stepped under the shower and sighed as the warm water cascaded over her aching body. Her mind detached for a moment and she caught herself swaying. The thought of what Logan would say if she pitched out of the tub galvanized her into finishing quickly. She dried herself and pulled the t-shirt on, shrugging over her lack of clean underwear. The soft hunter green tee fell almost to her knees. Wrapping herself in the robe, she emerged from the bathroom into the bedroom beyond, and wondered where she would be sleeping. Unwilling to just jump into what might be Logan's bed, she settled into the comfy wingback chair by the window and almost immediately dozed off.

* * * * *

Downstairs in the kitchen Dr. Maigrey was applying himself to a roast beef sandwich when Logan entered. He saluted Logan with his sandwich and swallowed. "Trust a lupine to have the best beef. You got this from Dave Newberry over in Sheraton County, didn't you?"

"Guilty. Nobody raises beef like Dave," Logan acknowledged. He seated himself at the table across from John. "Tell me."

"She was drugged," John stated baldly. "Did you notice that faint tangy odor?" At Logan's nod he continued. "It's a special mix of certain drugs and herbs. It's been making the rounds of the younger lupine set, who use it for a buzz. For our kind it's relatively harmless, considering our resistance to addictive substances. But for a human? Well, you saw the result."

"Son of a bitch." Logan's quiet wrath spelled trouble for the party responsible. John could almost feel sympathy for them. Almost.

"Luckily, it made her sick before it was completely absorbed into her system. Judging by the dilation of her pupils and the general disorientation and loss of motor function, I'd say that if she hadn't gotten rid of the contents of her stomach, that young woman could have been in serious condition right now."

Logan rose and began to pace the kitchen. "I'm going to kill that bitch," he swore.

"Who was it, Logan?" John kept his tone steady. He'd never seen Logan so close to losing control. The thought of what could happen was not good.

"Lillian Adair." He spit the name out like an oath. "She showed up while Bryn and I were having dinner at O'Neal's. She dropped her purse toward the end of her oh-so cordial visit. That had to be when she slipped that stuff into Bryn's tea. The rest of us were distracted picking her crap up off the floor. She and her friend Reece Cofield were the only other weres in the place, and he never got close enough to do the job, I'm sure of it."

"This is serious, Logan, but you can't go off half-cocked," John advised. "To make that kind of an accusation with no proof will bring nothing but trouble."

"I know," Logan conceded. "But I can't let this go unpunished."

"You'll think of something. For now, stay cool and use your head." He sighed and gathered up his bag, heading for the door. "I'm taking myself home to bed."

Logan clapped John on the shoulder. "Thanks, Doc, I really appreciate you coming." He paused thoughtfully. "And for the sound advice."

"No problem, Logan. Keep an eye on Bryn for the next couple of days. The only problem I anticipate may be stomach upset, and I left some pills upstairs on the nightstand. Keep her close just in case."

"Oh, I intend to keep her close," Logan grinned. "She's mine, my mate."

John was delighted. "Congratulations! She's unmarked. I had no idea."

"Neither does she. Yet," Logan confessed with a nervous laugh.

John chuckled. "Good luck, buddy. I get the feeling when she's more herself she's a feisty one."

"Oh yeah," Logan agreed. "My Bryn can be a real firecracker."

"Good for her. That just adds to the excitement." John paused, then solemnly intoned the formal words, "May you both enjoy the chase."

"Thank you, my friend," Logan replied, bidding John goodnight.

Logan locked up and returned upstairs, anxious to check on Bryn. He found her sound asleep in the wing chair in his bedroom. Quietly approaching her, he was pleased to see the return of faint color to her cheeks.

As he bent down and lifted her into his arms, she stirred, grumbling in irritation.

"Why didn't you get into bed, baby?" he asked softly.

"I didn't know where you wanted me," she mumbled, yawning.

"Under me would be good," he muttered.

"Hmm?"

Logan grinned. *Good thing she's so sleepy*, he thought. He put her down, sliding her out of his robe and into his bed. Turning the lights out he quickly undressed and joined her. A deep sigh of satisfaction passed his lips as Bryn immediately snuggled up to him. He gratefully acknowledged his body's willingness to let her presence in his bed go without having to fight off its normally insistent sexual urges. The worry he'd suffered, along with his protective instincts were apparently keeping his libido in check. He nuzzled his face in her hair, drifting off to sleep with the certain knowledge that Bryn was well and right where she was supposed to be.

A few hours later he wasn't so sure. Bryn began to squirm around and he woke, immediately solicitous. "Are you all right, baby?" he whispered, leaning over her. She pulled at the t-shirt she wore. "Hot, don't want this," she muttered as she struggled with it.

"Hold on, sweet, we'll get it off you." Logan took a deep breath and got the shirt untwisted, neatly pulling it over her head.

Bryn immediately quieted, drifting back to sleep. Logan immediately got a hard-on.

"Have mercy," he groaned reverently, swallowing.

Bryn lay stretched out in peaceful abandon. His superior night vision allowed him to see her quite clearly. Voluptuous was the word that came to mind. Her body was soft, rounded and curvy in all the right places.

He reached out and lightly cupped the full, firm swell of one breast. The nipple instantly beaded, pushing into the palm of his hand. He let his hand trail slowly down her abdomen. Her skin was smooth and warm, silk and satin under the slow glide of his fingers. Stopping to graze the soft curls at the apex of her shapely thighs, he paused as she stirred restlessly.

Hovering over her, he was mesmerized by her smell. His nose followed the trail his hand made as he breathed in the heady aroma of his mate. Arriving at her mound, he closed his eyes, inhaling deeply. He imagined parting the delicate folds, his tongue laving the swollen lips and the nectar-filled inner tissues. A low growl issued from his throat, bringing him back.

She's been sick, she's been sick, she's been sick, he repeated over and over, and with a heartfelt groan he removed his hand, pulling the covers back over her tempting body. Logan turned on his side with his back to her, hoping the removal of at least the visual part of the temptation would help.

His hope was short-lived. Bryn again nestled close. The twin peaks of her nipples burrowed into his back as her soft curves fitted against him. He could feel the brush of her pubic hair against his buttocks.

"Dear Lord," he groaned, and steeled himself to endure the rest of the night in frustrated torture.

* * * * *

Bryn woke abruptly, alone in the early morning. She climbed out of bed, groggy and confused, the vague notion of going home whirling in her brain. She shakily donned the robe that had been left at the foot of the bed and stood forlornly in the middle of the room, at a loss as to what to do next.

Having heard the faint movements upstairs, Logan arrived to check up on her. "Going somewhere, little girl?" he questioned fondly. She looked so sexy and yet so sweet, all sleepy and disheveled.

She ran an unsteady hand through her hair. "I thought I should go home...but I feel icky," she complained pettishly.

"Aw, baby, come here." Logan approached, holding out his arms. Bryn drifted into his embrace.

Sitting down on the edge of the bed, he settled her on his lap. "Do you hurt anywhere in particular?"

"My stomach hurts a little," she answered. "But I mostly just feel yucky all over." Her head rested on his shoulder.

"Doc left some stuff for your stomach." Logan indicated the bottle on the nightstand. "He thought you might need something. Let's get you back in bed." He lifted her up and reached for the tie on the robe she wore.

"Hey, hold on now," she said, taking an unsteady step back.

"Bryn, you know you don't like to sleep in anything, so you might as well shed the robe now," he pointed out reasonably.

She favored him with a fierce scowl. "*I* know I don't like to sleep in anything, but how do *you* know?" As soon as the question left her lips, the memory of his warm naked body pressed against her own sailed into her head. "You slept with me!" she accused.

"Yes I did," Logan admitted calmly. He fixed her with a serious, steady look. "You may as well get used to it, because it's going to be happening quite a bit from now on."

Her mouth opened, working, as incoherent noises emerged.

Logan tilted his head. "You look like a fish."

"You...you can't just *say* stuff like that," Bryn gasped, outraged.

"Well, honey, you were making fishy faces," he deliberately teased, and began working his own mouth in imitation.

"You know I meant that 'sleeping together' comment," she hissed.

Logan smiled, then considered her for a moment as she silently fumed. "Something special is happening between us, Bryn," he declared solemnly. "I know you feel it, just as I do." He waited expectantly for her acknowledgment. She nodded, a reluctant movement, but nevertheless an agreement. "I know this isn't easy for you, baby. Betrayal is not an easy thing to recover from. But Bryn—" Logan took her face in his hands, " —if you'll give me the benefit of the doubt, I'll prove you can trust me, just as I'm going to trust you." His lips tenderly brushed hers. "But for now, let's see about getting you well. Okay?"

"Okay," she agreed. Bryn found herself entranced by Logan. His obvious care *of* her and *for* her was disarming, and she found herself more and more willing to believe in him.

She took the pills he offered and drank them down with an entire glass of water, not realizing until then how thirsty she'd been.

"More?" he offered, indicating the water pitcher. "John said you need plenty of fluids."

"I think I've had enough for now. Thank you," she answered, then stood awkwardly, waiting for him to leave.

Logan smothered a smile. "I've seen you naked you know," he reminded her.

"Yeah, well, I haven't seen you see me naked, and if it's all the same to you, I'd just as soon delay that experience for a while." A rosy blush brightened her cheeks.

"Progress." Logan's affectionate smile and the tender heat in his eyes held Bryn captive.

"What?" she asked in a slightly distracted manner.

"You admitting we'll be naked together. I call that definite progress," he said, giving her a wicked wink.

Bryn felt a thrill stab through her midsection as a reluctant smile twitched her lips. "Go away, Logan," she ordered.

"I'm just downstairs if you need anything," he informed her with a grin. Placing a quick kiss on her lips, he left her to disrobe in private.

Bryn snuggled under the warm blankets. Sleepy contentment filled her being as the medicine settled her stomach. Yawning, she turned on her side and drifted off to sleep with a tiny smile on her lips.

Downstairs, Logan moved around the kitchen with practiced ease. He fixed coffee and made himself a ham and cheese omelet, all the while humming an off-key tune. His thoughts resided with the woman who even now warmed his bed.

Bryn was such an intriguing contrast. Sweet, shy, childlike and innocent, a wild sexy siren, at times exasperating, stubborn, spiritedly independent. She stimulated and challenged him as no other female had ever managed. His mind and body hummed with the flood of emotions she engendered in him.

Logan thought of his parents and knew unerringly that this was what they had, what they felt for each other. He knew how pleased they would be when he let them know he'd found his mate. His mother would probably cry, he thought with a smile. She was a bit emotional, just like Bryn, and he wouldn't change her for the world.

He considered calling them, then dismissed the notion. Better to wait until he broke the news to Bryn about his status as a werewolf. He exhaled a deep sigh. To say he was worried was an understatement. It would be a shocking revelation for Bryn to deal with. He was depending on her intelligence, her kind and caring personality, and the growing affection he knew she was feeling, to help her accept the truth of his dual nature.

He'd do whatever he had to, to help her accept the reality that was about to shatter all her preconceived notions. If, in the end, she rejected him, he'd have to let her go. But in doing so he would lose two crucial parts of himself that he would never recover—his heart and his soul.

Chapter Five

ଯ

Bryn woke to late afternoon sunshine and warm breezes spilling through the open windows. She sighed with the relief of feeling normal again and stretched luxuriously. Rolling to her side she snuggled into Logan's pillow and, catching his scent, pulled it close. A slow, pleased smile stretched her lips as she inhaled the masculine aroma.

Spurring herself into action, she rose from the bed and looked around curiously. Logan's bedroom. This certainly wasn't where she'd expected to end up last night when their date began. She admired the tall antique headboard of the bed as she ran her hand over the wood of the matching footboard. The dresser and bedside table — which was actually an old-fashioned washstand — matched the bed. All were substantial oak pieces with a deep honey-colored stain.

Thick, golden brown carpet cushioned her bare feet as she walked around. She glanced into the open closet to see Logan's clothes hanging inside. For some reason the sight made her insides flutter. Her inquisitive nature drew her to the open windows, which overlooked a huge backyard. A small fountain took center stage in a large, open grassy space surrounded by tall trees. The water splashed and sparkled in the sunshine as it spilled down a small waterfall and into a pool surrounded by mossy rocks. Bryn could just make out the sleek colorful shapes of the fish that swam there. Pulling herself away from the view, she decided a shower was in order. She started to grab the robe she'd worn before when she recognized the small open suitcase on the floor near the chair she'd first fallen asleep in.

A couple pairs of jeans and tops were laid out on the chair along with underclothes. Her toothbrush, hairbrush, shampoo and other toiletries were there as well.

Touched by Logan's consideration, she grabbed her stuff and quickly made use of the bathroom. Emerging clean and refreshed, she made her way downstairs, admiring the house as she went in search of Logan.

The rooms were decorated with an easy elegance that was warm and welcoming. Never one to pay much attention to decorating styles and periods, she still recognized that many of the pieces were cherished antiques. Their condition bespoke care and pride.

Hearing the murmur of voices, Bryn made her way down the hallway. She peeked hesitantly into the open door and discovered the den, Logan at his desk, but no one else in attendance.

He motioned her in. "Feeling better, baby?" he asked as he rose and came to her.

"Just fine, sweetheart," came a reply from the speakerphone in a very sarcastic, very male voice.

"Not you, you ass. Bryn just walked in." Logan gathered her close and pressed a slow warm kiss on her lips, which she eagerly reciprocated.

"I heard that," the voice informed them.

Walking her around the desk, Logan sat and urged her onto his lap. "Bryn, I'd like you to meet Jace McKenna. Lucky you can't see him, or I guarantee you'd be sick again."

Bryn snorted with suppressed laughter.

"Logan, you devil, you know if your lady saw me she'd throw you over so fast you wouldn't know what hit you. He's always been jealous of me, honey," Jace rejoined.

"I'm pleased to meet you, Jace," Bryn laughed. "I'm sure Logan's just exaggerating." She squirmed when he tickled her ribs in retaliation.

"Jace, will you be sure you spread the word about that matter we discussed?" Logan returned to business, eager to conclude matters so he could concentrate on Bryn.

Dr. Maigrey had called Jace, enlisting his help in spreading the word about what a certain drug, administered by an unknown person, had done to Logan's mate. Not one for gossip, John had felt it necessary to make the lupine community aware of the potential threat this drug had on their human neighbors.

Jace had called Logan, sure that Doc's discretion had kept him from revealing all the facts. Hearing of Lillian's perfidy was no surprise to him, in view of her known penchant for Logan.

"I will, Logan, we definitely don't want any more unpleasant incidents. I may let slip a bit of speculation, gleaned from an unknown source, if you know what I mean. That should make certain people alert to the fact that their actions haven't gone unnoticed. Bryn, it was nice speaking to you. I'm sure we'll meet in person real soon, and you'll see for yourself how much better looking I am than Logan."

"Dream on," Logan sneered and cut the connection.

After her dreadful night, the relief of being well and rested left Bryn feeling frisky She wrapped her arms around Logan's neck and proceeded to kiss him senseless.

Her lips explored his with slow, languorous teasing movements that had him simmering. When her tongue slid over his parted lips to ease inside, the heat began to churn. And when she suckled gently on his tongue as it played with hers, she sent him into a roiling boil.

She discovered the erection growing against her hip, and wiggled closer. The primal female reveled in her ability to incite his passion. She shivered at the feel of his hand as it ran down her side and over her hip to cup one taut, jean-clad buttock, kneading firmly.

"You *are* feeling better," he observed in a husky rasp.

"Much," she answered succinctly, eager to continue.

Just as her lips closed over his, a loud grumble sounded from her stomach. They both froze, eye to eye. Logan grinned and Bryn colored, embarrassed by her stomach's loud demands.

"I guess this means I should feed you before we address other hungers, hmm?" Logan's look was filled with heated promise.

"I could use something to eat," she confessed, rubbing her tummy. "After all, I did lose that wonderful supper you provided me with last night."

"Don't remind me," Logan admonished with a mock shudder. Rising from the chair he set her on her feet. "I had nightmares about that."

Bryn punched him in the arm as he drew away laughing. "I told you to leave, but nooo, you had to be all noble and stuff."

She followed him down the hallway and into the kitchen. Like all the other rooms it was beautifully designed. A butcher block-topped island centered the room. It was large enough that one end contained a sink while the other end held three chairs and could be used for casual dining. She admired the tumbled stone floor and ran a caressing hand over the smooth, green granite countertops. The cabinetry was all natural wood, the appliances built-in and unobtrusive.

"I've got some great roast beef here," Logan suggested, leaning in the open refrigerator. He turned to Bryn. "Sandwiches and coleslaw? Or there's some chicken stuff in the freezer I can nuke."

"The roast beef sounds great," she agreed, and stood by while he handed out all the fixings, which she deposited on the island. She watched him as he began to put things together. "You're pretty handy in the kitchen," she commented. "Where are the dishes?"

Logan directed her to them as he answered her observation. "A man needs to be able to take care of himself. My dad taught me that. Of course, that belief was encouraged by my mom," he added with a rueful smile.

"Where are your parents, Logan?" she inquired, taking up a knife and carefully slicing a tomato.

"In Scotland at the moment," he answered. "They travel a lot. When Dad retired they decided they wanted to see some of the places they'd read about." He paused. "Hot or cold?" he asked, indicating the plate of succulent roast beef.

"Hot, please." Bryn smiled. "This house is really beautiful, but isn't it awfully big for just you?"

As the beef warmed in the microwave, Logan spread mayo on slices of bread, handing them off to Bryn for the addition of lettuce and tomato. "This was Mom and Dad's home. There used to be five of us, including my sister and brother. As the eldest, they deeded this property to me and provided Kate and Dylan with properties of their own." He bent to bestow a lingering kiss on her lips. "Had you been a local girl, you would have known that."

Bryn savored his kiss and drew back, cocking an eyebrow at him. "I suppose all the local girls keep tabs on you?"

"Well, you know how it is…" Logan preened.

"Never mind, Mr. Modesty," she scoffed.

They continued to tease and banter through the meal and the cleanup, making for a pleasant, relaxing evening.

Hanging up the dishtowel after drying the last of the dishes, Bryn asked Logan a question that had been niggling at her since talking with Jace. "Logan, I know I'm being nosy, but is Jace one of the people you consult for? And what unpleasant incidents are you guys trying to avoid?"

Logan regarded her affectionately. "Yes, and you know that talk we need to have?" At her nod he continued, "Now's the time. Let's go back to my den and get comfortable."

Bryn followed him with some misgivings. She suspected this talk was going to cover some serious and sensitive issues. She just hoped that Logan wasn't into anything illegal.

Logan was struggling with some fairly large misgivings of his own. Now that the time had come to put the facts of his heritage before her, not to mention her role as his mate, he was more than a little worried. He knew she liked him and was sexually attracted to him, but he wanted more. He wanted her love — the love of one's mate was all-important, vital. Only through love would she be able to accept the wolf.

When he had discovered that she was the one, that first connection had been purely physical. Having spent time with her, he was learning the many facets that made up Bryn Royden. He found her fascinating, stimulating, intriguing — physically, mentally and emotionally.

With previous partners, he had enjoyed considerate and passionate physical encounters. With Bryn, Logan had gone beyond the physical connection. For the first time in his life, he found himself wanting more. His feelings had gone beyond caring and affection. He saw himself spending every day with her. Sharing his life with her. Having children with her. *Loving her.* The realization kicked him in the stomach like a runaway mule. The thought that she would be unable to accept his double nature, that she would spurn him, was intolerable. His future, whether a life filled with love, mate and family, or the bleak existence that would be his without her, rested in her hands. He'd never been in a situation where so much was out of his control. The feeling was alien and unsettling.

As they entered the den, Logan prayed that Bryn's feelings for him would be strong enough to let her accept what he revealed. He seated her on the sofa and himself on the coffee table, taking her hands in his. Looking deeply in her eyes he began. "The unpleasant incidents we want to avoid are ones like what happened to you last night. You were drugged, Bryn."

Confusion filled her eyes. "Drugged? But why, how?"

"Lillian Adair," Logan revealed, his tone clearly condemning. "The how, I suspect, was simply dumping the stuff in your tea at O'Neal's. Remember when she dropped her purse? We were all distracted. As to the why, petty jealousy. She's been trying to add me to her trophy case and I'm not cooperating. I'm really sorry, Bryn. She hurt you because of me."

Bryn could see anger mixed with contrition and — could it be? — anxiety. Surely he didn't think she would blame him? "It wasn't your fault," she consoled, squeezing his hands. "But shouldn't we report her to the police?"

Logan stood and began to pace. "There's just one problem with that, sweetheart. We have no proof. No witnesses, no 'she was caught red-handed with the evidence', no fingerprints on your glass, nothing. It would be our word against hers."

He settled in front of her, his eyes filled with a seriousness and concern she had never seen before. "There's another reason I wouldn't want to report this, even if we had proof." At Bryn's puzzled frown he continued, "It's because of *what* she is."

Tiny stirrings of unease began twisting inside her. "What do you mean, what she is?" Bryn questioned quietly.

"Lillian's a werewolf, Bryn. Just as I am."

Bryn stared at Logan as myriad emotions swirled inside. Amused disbelief came to the fore.

"You're a werewolf," she stated flatly. Sudden anger had her rising to her feet. "That sounds like the punch line, but I'm afraid I missed the joke." She began to pace as Logan regarded her silently. He couldn't possibly *believe* what he'd just told her. Why was he doing this? An aching hollow began to form inside her. Halting behind the sofa, she pinned Logan in her sights. Her voice shook with suppressed emotion. "You said I could trust you, and I believed you. I believed you, and all along you've just been waiting to make a fool of me." She paused, breathing hard, refusing the tears that threatened. "Well, you've succeeded. I just don't understand why. Why this elaborate ruse?"

Unable to wait for an answer, she turned blindly, unshed tears stinging her eyes. Hurt. Confusion. Anger. Disappointment. All roiled inside her like a pot set to boil. She strode for the door, desperate to be away from its source.

At the doorway Logan's hand wrapped around her wrist. "Don't go." His voice was quiet, controlled.

"Let go of me, Logan." Her even tone of voice did not betray the turmoil within.

"I can't, Bryn, you're my mate," he announced.

Her head shot up and without thought her palm cracked across his cheek with stinging impact. Bryn gasped, appalled disbelief holding her immobile. Shocked silence filled the room as they stared at each other.

Logan broke the silence, speaking flatly, without emotion. "I believe that entitles me to a few more minutes of your time."

Shame and remorse tore at her. Finally she nodded shakily, not knowing who to hate more, herself for her violent act, or him for provoking it.

Returning to their previous positions, they faced each other now as combatants. Logan regarded her silently, struggling to still the growing hurt and anger inside. "Years ago, when a wolf found his mate he took her. No explanations, no apologies. Females were required to submit. Now we seek to be civilized, to cajole and woo our mate. I'm an alpha." His voice dropped into a deep, gravel-like purr, the warning plainly evident. "In this situation there's only so much civilization I can stomach."

Bryn's eyes widened, uncertainty zipping through her. Could he possibly be telling the truth? Before her, his eyes took on an eerie glow. She could feel the waves of heat he generated and the intent plainly written on his face. She could also see the growing erection straining the fabric of his jeans. An involuntary wave of arousal spread inside as she found herself responding to his dominance. "What are you going to do?" She struggled to keep her voice even.

Logan acknowledged the slight quiver in her voice, his wolf appeased by her unconscious submission. "I'm going to prove that you can trust me. That I haven't lied to you. That I *am* a werewolf, and—" he leaned closer, sparks shooting within the glow of his eyes, "—that you *are* my mate. I'm going to change for you. Here. Now. Watch."

Bryn panicked. "Wait!" she yelped. "Wait, please, I need to know…"

"Need to know what?" he asked impatiently.

"Not that I believe anything's going to happen but—" she bit her lip, "—will you know me?"

Logan recognized her fear and uncertainty. His need to protect and comfort reasserted itself. He took her hand, threading his fingers through hers. "I'll know you, Bryn. We retain all awareness of self. Just in a different form."

Reassured by the return of his normal demeanor, she took the opportunity to question. "This isn't going to be like those old movies where the guy's face grows in slow motion, and claws form on his hands and stuff like that, is it? Because I always found that kind of gross."

The tension between them broke. Logan snorted with amusement. "No, it will happen very quickly. The whole wolf-man hybrid thing only happens if we consciously direct our power that way. Right now it will be just man, then wolf, in the blink of an eye." He smiled at her. "Ready?" At her nod, he moved the coffee table in front of the fireplace, making room.

Bryn followed Logan's every move and swallowed heavily as he stood before her and began to strip. "You have to take your clothes off, huh?" Her mouth suddenly felt extremely dry.

He nodded, a slow, sexy, self-satisfied movement that conveyed a wealth of meaning. Toeing off his boots, he set them aside. Bryn's gaze was captured as he opened the button on his fly and slowly lowered the zipper past the prominent bulge of his throbbing cock. She felt the heat of rising color in her face as she unconsciously squirmed on the sofa.

Having almost forgotten the main reason for this striptease, Bryn watched expectantly as the clothing came off. Even under these circumstances, Logan in the buff was a hell of a compensation.

He slowly unbuttoned his shirt, each open button revealing more of the muscular, lightly furred chest underneath. With graceful ease he pulled the tails of his shirt from his jeans and shrugged it off his wide shoulders, dropping it on the chair behind him.

Bryn sat glued to the sofa, fighting the urge to go to him. She watched the flexing play of muscle in his shoulders and arms as he hooked his thumbs in the waistband of his jeans and lowered them to the floor. The seemingly endless wait while those jeans slowly revealed hidden treasures was pure torture. Bryn felt parts of her body tighten with tension, while others grew hot, moist and open with growing arousal.

Logan straightened as his jeans hit the floor. Stepping free of them he stood, every orgasm-inducing, mouthwatering inch of his body proudly revealed.

"Holy shit, Batman," she whispered reverently. Her breath and heart rate began to speed as a hot flush swept her body.

The total package ravaged the senses. A Greek statue sculpted not in marble, but flesh, bone and muscle. And there at the center, demanding attention, was the longest, hardest, thickest cock she had ever seen. The long ivory column was wound with pulsing veins. The full plum-shaped head blushed with the blood that engorged the sensitive tissue. That proud, massive column could never hide under a fig leaf!

Captivated by his display, Bryn was eager to forget the whole werewolf thing and get on with the good stuff. She forced herself from Logan's cock and met his gaze. Her breath was momentarily arrested by the deepened glow of his eyes. Liquid gold, hot, burning, melting. Had she any idea of resisting his pull, what she saw there would have swept that intention away. Instead it ignited her passion, fueling her need, readying her for combustion.

"Ready?" he repeated, his voice a deep, hoarse growl.

Bryn shivered at the eager quiver in his voice. Knowing he awaited only her consent, her gaze again swept his body. Roused by the wave of heat that swept through her, she nodded.

Logan's image wavered, became indistinct, shimmered...changed. Bryn felt almost dizzy as her eyes tried to follow the blur of movement. She blinked, shook her head and refocused to find a huge wolf where Logan had stood.

She froze. As her sight grew dim she realized she'd forgotten to breathe. Sucking in air, wary of moving, her tongue came out to wet her dry lips. "Logan?" Her half whisper trembled on the air.

The wolf came slowly toward her and Bryn fought the overwhelming urge to run. Her breath rasped in her lungs as its muzzle drew closer to her face. Just as she thought she'd lose the battle to keep inside the terrified scream she held prisoner, a long rough tongue swept over her cheek.

She blinked in astonishment. "Logan?" she repeated. The wolf nuzzled her hand where it gripped her thigh. Tentatively, she raised her hand, placing it on his head and running it slowly down his neck. Staring into the depths of his golden eyes, undeniable recognition seeped in.

"Oh my god. It's you. It's really you." She gaped in fascination. "You're beautiful," she exclaimed softly with a teary laugh. Both hands now moved over and through the thick fur around his neck. She studied his face, noting the darker stylized markings around his eyes and muzzle. His thick coat was sleek and healthy, soft and smooth under her wandering hands. The upper part of his coat was the same dark sable of his hair, blended with gold and reddish highlights. It intermingled with the lighter color that flowed down his legs, chest and underbelly.

Bryn could feel the definition of sleek muscle under her hands. She marveled at the seemingly wild creature before her, knowing he would never hurt her. With that revelation came the knowledge of the power that he had placed in her hands. He trusted her. Logan trusted her with the knowledge of who and *what* he was.

She was flooded by a tidal wave of emotion. There were very few people in her life who trusted her and in whom she trusted. Her parents, her sister, Clare and Brian. In each case, love accompanied trust. Images of Logan, his words and actions over the past few days, flowed through her head. His kindness and caring, his smile, strength and intelligence, the passion he had for her, the passion he brought out in her for him. His words, "you're my mate", rang in her head. And now he gave his trust. His love.

"You're my mate." She spoke the words softly, wonderingly. Standing, she backed away from the wolf, pulling her shirt over her head. "You're my mate," she repeated boldly. "Change back. Change back now."

Her hands went to the button of her jeans, flipping it open. Sliding the zipper down, she stripped jeans and panties down in one long glide. Her gaze stayed with Logan until that disorienting shimmer of movement began. She unhooked her bra and dropped it with the rest of her clothes.

Logan stood before her, gloriously nude and fully erect. She launched herself into arms that wrapped her in heat, strength, protection and love.

"Logan, Logan, Logan." She chanted his name like a charm as she clung to him fiercely.

He threaded his hands in her hair, bringing them face-to-face. "Do you accept me?" he demanded. "All of me, Bryn?"

"Yes! All of you." Her own hands lifted, slid into his hair, twining, capturing him. "I love you and I want you, I need you now, Logan. Now."

Their mouths came together with savage intent as they fought to get closer. Her impassioned confession set

Logan aflame. The primitive need to mate filled his head with a red haze as he took them to the floor. They rolled, struggling for supremacy of position.

Logan pinned her to the carpet as his mouth explored her. He trailed teasing nips along her jaw and down her throat as she bounced and fought under him. Pleasure and frustration wrung moaning cries and whimpers from her throat as his mouth found her breast. His teeth fastened lightly on a hardened nipple as he suckled.

Bryn's nails bit into his shoulders as she surged under him. His mouth moved to her other breast to suckle with vigorous intent, causing her to arch up, biting his shoulder in reaction. A growl rumbled in the depths of his chest.

She pushed at him almost violently. "Let me," she gasped, and he gave in, rolling to his back.

Bryn attacked without hesitation. She laved the strong column of his throat with her tongue, nipping, licking, soothing. Her hand moved over his heaving chest, lightly pinching one masculine nipple. Her mouth settled over the other, her tongue making hot lazy circles around the hardened bud.

She drank in Logan's shuddering groan. He writhed under her ministrations and tensed as her hand trailed down his stomach to his groin. She wrapped her hand around the solid throbbing mast of his cock, squeezing strongly. His hips left the floor with a convulsive heave.

She felt an answering spasm as her pussy flooded with cream. Blind lust had her straddling his hips, preparing to ride his engorged shaft. Her channel felt open, aching to be filled. The pungent smell of her arousal filled the air.

"No." Logan's guttural command arrested her movement for a moment only. Her thighs tightened and she willfully ignored him until, with a twist of his big body, she again found herself pinned to the floor. She tried to wrestle free to no avail. With a snarl of defeat she acknowledged his superior strength.

"First time, my way," he growled darkly, rolling her to her stomach. She followed the unspoken instruction of his grip on her hips as he urged her to her hands and knees. His hard body blanketed hers. She felt seared by the heat his skin generated against hers. The hard ridge of his cock nestled in the cleft of her ass. The soft wiry hair of his chest brushed her back, making her shiver.

She felt the tightening of his body against hers as he pressed hard against her bottom. His deep panting groan filled her ear as his tongue swept inside to taunt and tease. Bryn tried and failed to swallow the anxious, tortured whimpers of need that ripped from her throat.

"Down," he ordered gruffly, putting pressure between her shoulder blades. She dropped to her elbows, leaving her bottom up. Her compliance brought a growl of approval and the slick sweep of his tongue as it trailed down the line of her spine. His teeth nipped a taut cheek, drawing a squeak of surprise from her. Bryn widened her thighs at his urging, feeling the fleeting brush of his hair as he knelt between them, bringing his mouth in contact with the swollen lips of her pussy. His tongue slid in, swirling in the thickened petals of her sex, stirring the bewitching scent of her arousal.

Bryn came up off her elbows on a keening moan which became a startled gasp as Logan's palm landed on her upturned bottom with a resounding smack.

"Down," he ordered again, his voice hard. The alpha would tolerate no disobedience.

Whimpering, she obeyed, dropping down in submission. Her thighs quivered in anticipation and she jumped as she felt him blow a warm breath against her dripping cunt. Gentle fingers firmly parted her nether lips and again his tongue began the sweet torture.

Bryn cried out, her fingers curling into fists as she sought something to hold onto. The slick sweep of Logan's tongue against her ultra-sensitive folds drove her higher and higher. He alternated sucking her clit and drilling his stiffened tongue inside her wet channel until she was a mass of quivering flesh, balanced on the edge of madness.

Logan drank Bryn's nectar as it flowed from his ministrations. He was intoxicated by her taste and scent. Her frantic cries and the pounding demand of his throbbing cock penetrated his consciousness. He rose over her, positioning the plump head of his cock at her streaming entrance. A quick, shallow thrust saw the head wedged inside as he again covered her.

"My mate," he growled harshly, possessively. "Mine." Biting down on her shoulder, he thrust.

Slick fluid gushed, displaced by the tunneling invader. Bryn's wail of pleasure rang out as his thick cock slid deeper and deeper until every inch was buried inside. Her slick channel welcomed him. First stretching and quivering to accommodate, then tightening, squeezing. He slowly rocked against her, forward and back, long deep strokes. She pushed back hard, encouraging, demanding more.

Logan began a deep pounding rhythm that sent his cock surging repeatedly into her clasping depths. Thrust, retreat, thrust, retreat. Mindlessly, endlessly, again and again. Both were lost in the primal heat of their mating. Grunts of effort accompanied the steady slap of flesh meeting flesh. Gleaming, heated skin shone with sweat under the lamplight. The rounded, fleshy mounds of Bryn's bottom jiggled with each forward drive of Logan's hips. The heavy weight of his seed-laden balls rhythmically smacked her cunt. Each pumping stroke brought the pulsing head of his driving shaft in contact with her cervix. Her moans of approval accompanied the grinding of her hips as she strained against him for more.

He drove them higher, until they balanced on the precipice of a pleasure so sharp as to be borderline pain. Her tightening pussy and frenzied cries announced her impending orgasm. Logan reached down, moistening his fingertips in her juices. Finding her clit, he applied gentle pressure, rubbing the hardened nub, sending Bryn screaming over the edge. Trapped in the vise of her clutching, engorged channel, his beleaguered member exploded. He uttered an intense guttural growl, shoving deep, as stream after stream of thick, hot seed coated her quivering vaginal walls. Release-weakened muscles encouraged their collapse to the floor.

Bryn continued to emit small whimpering cries as descending ripples of orgasm milked the hard shaft buried in her pussy. Logan's crooning murmurs soothed her as he snaked his arms around her and carefully rolled their joined bodies on their sides. He pulled her upper leg up and over his own. One hand closed over her breast, rubbing the elongated nipple against his palm. His other hand slid sensuously down her moist satiny skin. It skimmed over the gentle swell of her belly to cup her drenched pussy, which still hosted his semi-erect penis.

He gently massaged the engorged lips of her cunt. His middle and ring finger parted in a fork to enclose his cock, which began to fill and lengthen as he lightly pinched her swollen lips around the thickening shaft. With the heel of his hand he applied pressure to the sensitized nub of her clit. Hidden under her labia, it still transmitted shockwaves of pleasure.

Bryn trembled and moaned at the caress. She gasped as Logan began a slow measured stroke.

"Again," he breathed in her ear.

A shiver ran down her spine as he nibbled her earlobe. He tongued the sensitive skin under her ear. The hand enclosing her breast squeezed and kneaded that tender flesh. His fingers found the distended nipple, lightly pinching and pulling. His cock, now fully engorged, sawed in and out of her cunt.

Time ceased to exist as he plundered her pliant, welcoming flesh. She could no longer differentiate between the touch of his hands or lips or tongue and the slide of his cock. Closing her eyes she gave herself up to pure raw sensation.

Logan drank in his mate's cries of pleasure. The pungent scent of sex filled his nostrils as her flesh filled his hands. He curled his body around hers, thrusting with determined vigor. The unmistakable tingle of pending release fluttered at the base of his spine. He opened the pouting lips of her sex wider. Bathing his fingers in the thick cream he found there, he glided them softly, again and again, over her raw clit. Her body stiffened, then convulsed against him as she exploded into orgasm. Her wailing cry, laden with agonized pleasure, rent the air.

Logan grasped her hips, grunting with each thrust that pounded into her tight channel. Driven by instinct, he again fastened his teeth into the soft flesh between neck and shoulder, holding her still for his driving thrusts. Pulsing waves of cum rocketed down his shaft, erupting into her welcoming heat.

Spent, they lay spooned together. Minutes passed without notice. Heartbeats slowed. Tension drained from exerted muscles. Breaths, once harsh and panting, grew smooth and even. Sweat cooled and dried. Bryn sighed, shivered.

Logan's arms tightened around her. "Cold?" he asked.

"Uh-uh," she replied, snuggling back in his embrace. "Logan?"

"Mmmm?" he gave a drowsy rumble.

"You bit me."

"Uh-huh," he agreed.

"Am I going become a werewolf?" she asked.

"Uh-uh," he denied.

"Oh." Disappointment tinged her voice.

Logan leaned up on his elbow, looming over her. She leaned back to meet his eyes then turned over to face him.

"Do you *want* to become a werewolf?" he asked her seriously.

"Well," she began, running her fingers idly over the carpet. "You know how you imagine something, never really dreaming it's possible?"

At his nod she continued. "That's what I did. I've read books and imagined what it would be like to be a vampire or a werewolf or a shape-shifter of some kind, or have magical powers. Does that sound weird?" she asked, looking up at him, hesitant, shy.

Logan smiled. "Not at all." He reached out to brush a strand of hair behind her ear. "You have an open mind when it comes to otherworldly possibilities. Considering the circumstances, that turns out to be a very good thing."

Bryn returned his smile. "Anyway, I was thinking that if you biting me — which seems to be the standard way a human is turned into a werewolf — turned me, it would be okay." Her look turned pensive. "But I guess it's not possible."

Logan considered her for a moment. "It's possible," he confessed.

"It is?" Bryn sat up, her breasts jiggling with her excitement. "How?"

Tearing his eyes from her protruding nipples, he offered a suggestion. "How about we get cleaned up and get you covered up before I jump you again? Then maybe I can cover the details without drooling."

She grinned and reached for the shirt he'd left draped over the chair. Standing, she pulled it on, fastening the most strategic buttons. "Better?"

"Some," he grumbled.

"Come on," she encouraged. "I'll race you to the shower."

With a laugh she raced out of the room. Logan sprang to his feet and followed. Pounding footsteps echoed on the stairs. She squealed as he caught her at the bedroom door and with a growl he swung her up and over his shoulder, carrying his giggling, wriggling prize into the bathroom.

* * * * *

Lukewarm water sloshed lazily in the filled tub. Its silky glide cooled overheated skin and washed away the remnants of sexual play. After catching his mate, his libido stimulated by the chase, Logan had taken Bryn again. A hard, fast fuck while bent over the bathroom counter left them both weak-kneed and breathless. The eye contact they had maintained via their reflection in the long mirror had been electrifying. The physical stimulation enhanced by the visual of Bryn's breasts bouncing as Logan speared into her again and again had them exploding hard and fast.

Seated between his spread thighs, her back to his chest, Bryn drifted on a cloud of sated contentment. Her arms rested along the rim of the tub, while his circled her abdomen. "I forgot to thank you for bringing some of my clothes and things over while I was asleep," she murmured lazily.

"I didn't. It was Clare," he informed her, his voice a deep, sleepy drawl.

"Oh my god, Clare! I forgot Clare!" Bryn struggled to sit up, a useless gesture as Logan's arms tightened like steel bands around her middle.

"Relax, she knows where you are." He leaned forward to nuzzle her shoulder. "I called her while you were sleeping. She brought your things and even came upstairs to see you, but you were so deeply asleep she didn't want to wake you." With his explanation, Bryn stilled, relaxing in his arms. "You can call her in the morning." His warm breath ghosted across her neck and shoulder, .causing a tiny shiver. His tongue began slow laving strokes over the small wounds caused by his incisors where they had gripped her. "Does it hurt?" he questioned softly, examining the wounds with a combination of pride and regret. Pride that she wore his mark, regret for hurting her.

She quivered under the solicitous laps of his tongue. "Mmmm, no," she breathed. "If you don't stop that, I'm going to need that clever tongue in other places. Soon."

"I'll be more than happy to accommodate you, sweet," he replied with eager heat.

Her hands came up, caressing his head as her fingers slid into the silky mass of his hair, took a firm grip and pulled.

"Ow, what did you do that for?" He pulled back reflexively and she let him go.

"No more playtime until you answer a few questions," she stated in a decisive tone.

"Fine," he muttered sulkily, rubbing his abused scalp. "As long as I get to keep my hair. How would it look for an alpha to have a bald spot? I'd be laughed out of the pack."

"Oh, you big baby," she scoffed. She turned, rising to her knees to face him. Cupping his head in her hands she nuzzled her face into his hair, placing small solicitous kisses over his abused scalp. Her hands wandered down to his cheeks, pulling his face up to hers. Sudden tears filled her eyes.

"Hey, I was just joking, you didn't hurt me," Logan soothed.

"I hit you." Her breath hitched in her throat. "Earlier, I didn't believe you and I hit you. I'm so sorry, Logan. Will you forgive me?"

Logan gathered her in, the feel of her wet naked flesh against his own making him want to groan. "There's nothing to forgive, sweetheart. It was the shock. I know you didn't mean it." He rubbed her back, his hand trailing down to cup one firm buttock. "Besides, we're even. I hit you, too."

She drew back. "You mean when you, when we were...?" A heated blush suffused her cheeks.

Logan nodded, a wry smile on his lips.

"That was...okay." She dropped her head, avoiding eye contact.

Dawning comprehension lit his eyes. "You liked it," he stated smugly. He tilted her head up to meet his gaze. "Does my naughty little girl like to be spanked?" The smoky rumble of his voice caused her pussy to clench.

"No, and stop that!" she exclaimed, as she scrambled to her feet and stepped out of the tub. Uncontrollable excitement squeezed her insides as she grabbed a towel and briskly began to dry off.

Logan followed suit. Drying himself, he sidled up to her back. "I can smell your excitement, Bryn," he teased.

She whirled on him and he stepped back, holding up his hands in capitulation at the sparks that shot from her eyes. "It's not funny!" she shouted, then turned away murmuring, "It's sick", the dismay clearly evident in her voice.

Without warning, Logan scooped her up and strode into the bedroom. Dropping her on the bed, he swooped down and pinned her protesting body under his. "Stop squirming," he ordered. Capturing her wrists in one hand, he pinned them above her head. His lower body cradled between her thighs, he rose over her. "Look at me," he demanded. Defeated, she raised shame-filled eyes to his.

A gentle smile filled with understanding curved his lips. "It's not sick," he comforted. "It's kinky. I love it."

As his declaration sank in, Bryn frowned. "Are you sure? I've never done, you know, stuff like that. But I've read a lot about it and it's, ah, stimulating. It makes me..." She wiggled under him.

"Horny?" he supplied with a grin.

"Yeah," she admitted with a reluctant quirk of her lips.

"This is beautiful," Logan rhapsodized. "My sweet, beautiful, intelligent, sexy mate wants to be dominated." He growled fiercely. "Remember I told you I'm an alpha?" At her nod he continued, "Alphas dominate, it's our nature." Lowering his head to her abdomen he teased her with licks and nips that had her giggling and squirming under him.

Sobering, he captured her gaze with his. A soft glow began in his eyes. "There's something I've always wanted to try," he confessed.

Bryn's eyes widened with some apprehension but most of all anticipation. "What?" she questioned breathlessly.

"It involves you," he elaborated, "totally naked, except for a hooded red cloak."

Bryn dissolved into snickering giggles.

"Aw, come on," Logan urged. "I've always wanted to play the big, bad wolf."

"No!" she laughed.

"Seriously, you and me in the woods." He wiggled his eyebrows with lascivious intent. "It could be fun. I promise I'll eat you..." he cajoled.

She totally lost it, laughing until tears coursed down her cheeks. Logan waited, a disgruntled look on his face. "It wasn't *that* funny," he groused, levering himself up and off her.

Bryn struggled to sober up. She sat up, throwing her arms around him. "Aw, honey, don't be mad," she cooed. "If it means that much to you, I'll think about it." She ducked her head under his, trying to capture his attention. "Okay?"

"Okay," he grumbled. His eyes met hers and, as a slow, sexy grin crossed his face, he winked.

"You rat!" she huffed, shoving him backward. "You were just teasing me!"

Logan bounced on the bed, landing on his back. "Gotcha," he laughed. "By the way, that's wolf, not rat. Wererat, that's a whole 'nother animal."

She glared at him suspiciously. "Do you mean to tell me there are *wererats*?"

"Anything's possible," he replied with a shrug. "You never knew about the existence of werewolves until a few hours ago. Never limit the possibilities," he advised. "It's unwise."

She acknowledged his philosophy with a nod. "Speaking of werewolves," she said, steering back to the subject she'd originally wanted to speak to him about. "You were going to tell me how you can make me one."

Logan rolled to his side and regarded her seriously. "It's only possible when the female of the mated pair is fertile and ready to conceive a cub." At her shocked look, he amended, "A *child*, and no, you wouldn't have a wolf cub," he reassured. "We werewolves have a heightened sense of smell. I'll be able to detect when you're ovulating.

It will trigger the release of, for lack of a better term, the werewolf gene into my saliva. If, at that time, we mate, my bite will transfer the gene to you and you'll become a werewolf. In the case of a female werewolf with a human male, she's the one who would do the biting, transforming her mate."

He sat up, taking her hands in his. "It's a big decision, Bryn. It only happens at this time because wanting to create a child together proves the pair's commitment to each other. It's also a safety net for werewolves who have casual relationships with humans. It allows us to have sex without turning every partner we have into a werewolf, if biting becomes part of the sex. It's not always. It depends on the partner and how much emotion and passion is involved. It's not something to be taken lightly. For us it's the ultimate commitment. Unlike humans, we mate for life."

"I don't want to get pregnant every time I ovulate," Bryn said worriedly.

He smiled indulgently. "You won't. We werewolves are just as informed about birth control methods as the average person. We'll lay in a big supply of condoms," he teased. "From what I understand, when you're fertile I won't be able to keep my hands off you. I may have you in bed during the whole cycle."

Bryn flushed with pleasure. "That shouldn't be too hard to endure." She leaned forward, placing a warm kiss on his willing lips. "I have another question." At his nod she proceeded. "What's to keep a werewolf from mating with a fertile woman and biting her even if they're not committed?"

"Aroma," he answered. "Just as our sense of smell is what first leads us to our mates, it's also what keeps us from mating with a fertile female who is not ours. The fertile smell of one's own mate is said to be intoxicating. But the smell of one who is not?" Logan wrinkled his nose. "It's actually rather repugnant. Believe me, I know this from firsthand experience. Have you ever tried having sex with someone who smells bad to you?" he questioned. At the negative shake of her head he explained, "It's pretty much impossible to get an erection, much less maintain one, when your nose is screaming at you to run."

Bryn chuckled. A suspicious gleam lit her eyes. "You mean you knew I was your mate because of how I *smell*?"

He laughed. "I wondered if you'd pick up on that. Yes, I did," he admitted.

"So," she asked self-consciously, "how do I smell?"

Logan closed his eyes, inhaled, then breathed out slowly. "Bewitching." His eyes captured hers. "Warm, sweet, fresh, succulent, like an exotic spice for which there is no name." He brought her hands to his lips, placing a kiss in each palm. "You smell like my mate. Without question. Without doubt. Mine." His eyes glowed with the inner fire she was beginning to find so exhilarating. "Any more questions?" he asked softly.

Bryn's heart swelled with his words, the ache in her chest warm and welcome. "Just one," she answered. "We've made love three times now, and each time you were behind me. Do werewolves ever make love face-to-face?"

"Oh yeah," he growled.

She lay back, opening herself to him. "Come here and love me."

Logan lowered himself between her thighs, sinking slowly inside her hot, flooded sheath. "I do, Bryn," he groaned. "I do love you."

Chapter Six

ဆာ

Logan looked fondly down upon his sleeping mate. Tousled blonde hair spilled across the pillows in tangled disarray. A soft blush tinted her cheeks, and her reddened lips were swollen and slightly parted, soft, even breaths issuing forth. The voluptuous form that had driven him nearly insensible with lust last night was outlined under a rumpled sheet.

He'd been hard-pressed to keep his hands off her. Each time he loved her only made him want her that much more. His unruly member had stayed semi-erect the entire night. Even after filling her with his seed he'd remained immersed in her body, dozing fitfully only to awaken, rock-hard, buried deep in her slick, hot pussy. The need to fuck her, to possess her, to master her, rode him like an ingrained compulsion. She had to be shown without a doubt that she belonged to him. That he was her alpha and her mate.

Twice in the den, once in the bathroom, three times through the night and early morning hours and once again this morning before he'd risen to shower. They'd made love seven times, no wonder she was exhausted. Logan was a little amazed himself.

He, on the other hand, felt invigorated, renewed. His mate! Her presence filled him with wonder and joy. He was beginning a whole new chapter in his life and looking forward to every page, every sentence.

He leaned down, inhaling her warm mesmerizing scent, while placing a chaste kiss on her cheek.

Bryn stirred, mumbling, "No more, too tired."

"Shh, go to sleep, baby," he whispered. Straightening, he tucked the covers securely around her and headed downstairs.

* * * * *

A couple of hours later, Logan sat in his den contemplating his conversation with Jace. Born into Iron Tower pack, Logan was required to introduce his new mate to his fellow pack members. He and Jace had decided to introduce Bryn at the Iron Tower-Twin Pines pack meet that was scheduled for three weeks from today.

Jace, Logan and, amazingly enough, Charles Delancy, alpha of the Twin Pines pack, had decided that having a semiannual meeting combining the members of both packs might help keep trouble to a minimum. The members of both packs, once familiar with each other, were more inclined to avoid petty squabbles and challenges.

None of the men anticipated any problems. Logan's status assured her acceptance, and Bryn herself, used to dealing with the public, was no shrinking violet. He was sure she'd hold her own, despite being surrounded by a bunch of strangers who also just happened to be werewolves.

Logan's attention was drawn to the window. An unfamiliar vehicle was approaching the house. He reached the front door and opened it just as the engine died. Reece Cofield stepped out.

His senses went into immediate overdrive. With Bryn upstairs, any unfamiliar male was viewed as a threat, doubly so if that male was another werewolf.

Reece approached slowly, projecting as unthreatening a presence as possible. "May I speak with you, Logan? I offer no challenge, present no threat." His words were uttered with nervous determination.

Relaxing slightly, Logan waved him inside. Keeping Reece in front of him and his movements under strict observation, he motioned him into his den. "Sit," he offered, indicating the sofa. Logan sat on the edge of one of the chairs, the coffee table between them. "What did you want to see me about?" he questioned.

"It's about what happened to your mate," Reece answered. Seeing the tension tighten Logan's muscles, he quickly forged on. "I just wanted you to know that I had no hand in it. Word's going round that she was given something at O'Neal's. Word also is that what she was given is something accessible only to weres, and as Lillian and I were the only others present that night, it had to have been one or the other of us that gave it to her."

He took a deep breath, forcing his eyes to meet Logan's. "I don't do drugs, Logan, and I don't give them to anyone else, for any reason."

Logan met his look until Reece dropped his eyes. "I never suspected you," he conceded. "Lillian's the culprit. I think we both know why."

Reece nodded. "Yeah, Lillian has this thing for you." His voice was filled with bitter defeat. "I'll be going now, thanks for listening."

"Hold on, Reece," Logan ordered. "You care about her."

"For all the good it does, yeah, I love her." Reece stood and went to the window, staring out. "I know Lillian's a royal pain in the ass, but she's got issues nobody knows about. Her mother died when she was young and her dad's an autocratic asshole with an ice cube for a heart. I've met him. The way he treated her, it was all I could do not to dropkick the fucker into next week."

At Logan's murmur of understanding, he turned from the window. Rubbing the tightened muscles at the back of his neck he continued, "I know it's not an excuse for her behavior, lots of people make it past a rotten childhood. Lillian's sister is one of the sweetest people you could ever meet. Happily married, with a couple of cubs." A look of hopeless resignation crossed his face. "Lillian's not happy. If she'd only look at what's in front of her instead of…" he paused, looking at Logan. "I know I could make her happy if she'd just give me a chance."

"Make her," Logan stated. Seeing Reece's look of puzzlement, he explained, "Lillian's a strong woman, she needs a stronger man. How long have you been seeing her?"

"Five months now," he answered.

Logan raised his eyebrows. "I'm impressed. I've never known Lillian to hang on to a man for more than a few weeks before giving him the heave-ho. She likes you. Could be she feels more than that, but being Lillian, she needs a strong man, a dominant mate."

"I see what you're getting at," Reece conceded. "But what can I do?"

Logan rose. Going to Reece, he slapped him on the shoulder. "For starters, I have a gym in the basement. Starting tomorrow you're to be here every day. Expect to spend a couple of hours. There's nothing like some added muscle to build a man's confidence." He led Reece to the front door. "And while you're building that muscle, I'm going to share some lessons with you that my father—a very wise alpha, I might add—shared with me."

Reece held out his hand, which Logan took, shaking firmly. "Thanks, Logan."

"Don't thank me, my motive's not entirely altruistic. Lillian's name crops up in half the disputes I have to smooth over. If you make her happy—" he grinned, "— my job is going to be so much easier."

Reece laughed. "Well, whatever the reason, you still have my thanks and my promise to get Lillian off your back."

"Good enough," Logan replied. "Tomorrow, nine a.m."

He closed the door and turned to see Bryn making her way carefully down the stairs. He noted the slight stiffness of her movements with a knowing, unrepentant smile. When she made the bottom step he took her carefully in his arms, tilting her head up for a long warm kiss. "Hi," he murmured against her lips.

"Hi," she replied softly, her eyes wide, brimming with love.

"You're walking a little gingerly this morning, sweet. Sore?" His solicitous question was offset by the teasing light in his eyes.

"Guess whose fault that is?" she accused tartly, a blush staining her cheeks.

"I hope you're not trying to implicate me," Logan declared with false outrage. "After all, I'm not the sweet, lush morsel who kept moaning in my bed all night, tempting and teasing."

"No, you're the insatiable sex maniac that kept the morsel moaning," she shot back.

Logan squeezed her tenderly. His look turned contrite. "I'm sorry, baby. Was I too rough?"

His tender concern warmed her heart. "Not really, I just wasn't in shape for a lovemaking marathon. It's been awhile since I've done this kind of thing. Heck, who am I kidding," she admitted with a self-deprecating grimace. "I've never done this kind of thing before." She took his face in her hands. "You're an amazing lover. I couldn't get enough."

Logan's heart flipped over in his chest. "You sure know how to stroke a man's ego, sweetheart," he praised. "As well as other things." His mouth took hers in a tender kiss that heated their blood.

Bryn pulled back, breathless. "Tell you what," she offered. "All's forgiven if you'll..." She gave him a seductive look.

"What?" That look had Logan ready to agree to anything.

"Feed me," she smiled. "I'm starving."

"Vixen." His arm looped over her shoulder as he steered her toward the kitchen. "Guess I should feed you, keep your strength up for the next round."

"Har, har," she quipped, then yelped as he pinched her bottom as she pushed open the kitchen door.

* * * * *

After lunch, they retreated to Logan's den. As it was Sunday, Bryn called Clare at home, eager to reassure her friend that all was well. Logan lazed on the sofa, half-closed eyes sparkling, smiling indulgently as Bryn giggled with Clare over the phone. Even grown women reverted to a teenage mentality when a new man entered their lives. He yawned. Last night's excesses had had some effect on him after all. Logan dozed off to the soothing murmur of Bryn's voice.

He woke to a tickling sensation on his nose. Without opening his eyes, he reached out and pulled a teasing Bryn on top of him. "Nap with me," he rumbled. There was plenty of room on the wide sofa. He settled her against his chest, her head tucked under his chin, her limbs tangled with his. They both sighed with contentment and drifted off to sleep.

An hour later the jangling ring of the telephone had Bryn jumping with alarm. Logan caught her just as she started to roll off him and onto the floor. "Easy, sweetheart," he crooned, his voice husky with sleep.

He sat up and, placing a groggy Bryn securely on the sofa, made a dash for the phone.

"Sutherland," he answered briskly. He listened intently for a few moments. "Yeah, I know that. You and Farrell assured me you had it under control." Again he listened to the speaker on the other end of the line. "All right, look, try to keep a lid on it. I can be there in a few hours. Meet me at the landing strip in Tuskero." Another spate of conversation came through. "We'll see when I get there, all right? All right." He hung up the phone and looked at Bryn. "I've got a job."

"One of your consultations?" she asked.

"Yeah, come upstairs with me and I'll explain while I pack."

Bryn agreed and together they went upstairs. She sat on the bed while Logan packed a couple changes of clothes and other necessities in a duffel bag. As he packed he explained his job to her, and the new problem that had come his way. Two neighboring packs were having a disagreement over their territorial line. An actual fight had ensued, but the combatants had been forcibly separated by their alphas, who were just managing to keep their respective packs in check. The alphas themselves were quickly losing their desire to avoid bloodshed as the instinctive lure of the wolf's way pushed them to act.

"So this dispute you're mediating is in Montana?" she asked.

"Yeah, and I can't spare the time to drive. I keep a Cessna at the local airstrip here so I can make quick flights without having to depend on commercial airplanes. It's easier this way," he explained.

"You know how to fly a plane?" Bryn was amazed at all the new facets of Logan she was discovering.

"I sure do. If you're a good girl while I'm gone, I'll take you for a ride when I get back," he winked, offering the bribe. He disappeared into the bathroom to gather his toothbrush and shaving kit. Bryn heard the sound of the toilet lid come up and liquid hitting liquid. She smiled at Logan's unselfconscious action. In a way it was oddly comforting. Following the flush of the toilet and water running in the sink, he emerged from the bathroom, adding his personal grooming items to his bag.

"I think I'll go home while you're gone," Bryn announced.

"You're welcome to stay here, you know that, don't you?"

"I know, but I'll feel uneasy without you here," she explained. "Anyway, it'll be easier for me to be home since all my stuff's there. I'll be going in to work tomorrow, so I'll need my car, too."

"Can you get home all right?" Logan asked, his concern apparent. "If you want, I'll wait while you pack and drop you home on my way out of town."

"No need, I can get home okay. I'll call Clare. Or better yet, I'll just call a cab. That way I won't drag her away from whatever she and Brian are doing," she reconsidered.

Logan nodded. She could see his mind was already moving to what state of affairs would be waiting for him in Montana. As he grabbed his bag and headed downstairs, Bryn trailed forlornly behind. At the front door Logan dropped the bag, turned and found Bryn biting her lip, her eyes shiny with welling tears. He opened his arms and she stepped into the warm shelter he provided.

"Don't cry, sweetheart. I'll be back in a couple of days."

He felt her nod against his shoulder.

"I'm sorry I'm being a big baby. It's just that we just got started and you're going and I'll *miss* you."

He drew back, capturing her gaze. "I'll miss you too, baby. Look at it this way," he pointed out, "now you've got a couple of days to recuperate." His gaze turned sultry. "Take some hot baths. Get limbered up for when I get back."

Bryn laughed and threw her arms around his neck, hugging him fiercely. "I'll do that," she agreed, then sobered, her eyes becoming soft pools of misty gray. "Be careful."

His golden brown eyes melted into pools of amber heat. "Don't worry about me, I'll be fine." His arms tightened around her, holding her close. "I know we've, as you put it, 'just got started', but when I get back, we are having a serious discussion about you and me."

"Another serious discussion? I think I'm scared." Her tremulous smile countered her teasing words.

Logan's hand trailed down, patting her softly on her rounded bottom. "Don't be a smartass little girl, or I'll have to spank you."

"Logan..." Bryn felt immediate arousal at his tantalizing words.

He captured her mouth in a feral kiss, his tongue sweeping in to pillage and plunder. He swallowed Bryn's moan as she was swept away by his passionate onslaught. After thoroughly exploring her willing mouth he broke the kiss, whispering a sensual promise. "We'll discuss *that* when I get home, too." With a final devastating kiss and a firm pat on her bottom, he headed out.

Bryn watched him, waving as he drove down the driveway. She closed the door and leaned against it. With a gusty sigh and a bemused smile, she headed to the den to call a cab.

* * * * *

A couple of days later, after a hectic day at the store, Bryn was home relaxing on the sofa. Having just showered, she was dressed in a soft pink t-shirt and her favorite flannel teddy bear boxers. An empty container of pasta salad and a half-full glass of lemonade rested on the coffee table. On the television, the weatherman spouted his forecast with confident aplomb.

She stretched and yawned, then regarded the empty pasta container with a scowl, wondering if she wanted to expend the energy to get up and throw it away or continue to play couch potato. The sudden shrill ring of the phone saved her the trouble of deciding.

Bryn hesitated, a pensive frown crossing her features. It had to be Logan. He'd called her every night he was away and last night he had been certain that one more day would see his business concluded. No way to avoid it, she had to wiggle her way out of seeing him tonight if he was back.

Picking up the phone, she answered with a soft "Hello?"

"Hi, baby, it's me." Logan's voice, deep and rich, sent a thrill through her middle.

"Logan." She exhaled a small breathy sigh. "Are you back?"

"I sure am, sweetheart. I'm about ten minutes away. Grab some clothes and what ever else you need. I'll pick you up and we'll head over to my house." There was a pregnant pause. "I got plans for you, babe."

The sensual heat in his voice sent a shiver through Bryn. She grimaced, wanting to screech with frustration. Keeping her voice level she replied, "I can't tonight, Logan. We had a really crazy day at the store today and I'm exhausted. Can we make it tomorrow?" She crossed her fingers, hoping things would be back to normal by then.

"What's wrong, Bryn?"

"Nothing." She strove to project a casual, natural tone. "I'm just tired."

"Okay, that's fine, but you can still come home with me." His voice became soft, persuasive. "I've missed you, Bryn. I want you with me. I need to hold you, baby."

Her insides quivered with not only physical need, but emotional need as well. "Logan, I really want to, but I need to stay here. Just one more night. I promise we'll be together tomorrow." Bryn closed her eyes, rocking with nervous agitation, her toes curling into the carpet.

"Bryn, you haven't changed your mind, have you? About us?" His hurt was more than apparent coming over the phone line.

Bryn rushed to reassure him. "No, Logan! I just need to stay here one more night."

"Why?" His voice turned dangerously soft.

"I can't explain it," she hedged.

"You *will* explain it," he ordered, exasperation making his tone sharp.

Her temper flared. "I told you I can't and I won't!"

Logan's own temper burst. "I'll be there in five minutes and you *will* tell me what the hell is going on!"

He broke the connection and Bryn stood, stamping her feet and cussing like a trucker. Five minutes later Logan's car pulled into the driveway. Seconds later he was pounding on the door.

"Bryn, open the door," he demanded.

"Go *away*, Logan," she insisted.

"I will break this door down, Bryn. You have ten seconds." The deadly earnest tone of his voice broke her resolve.

The door was unlocked and thrown open. "Fine, it's open! I hope you're happy now!" She stamped away, leaving him in the open doorway.

Slamming the door shut, Logan strode after her, grabbed her arm in a firm but careful grip and swung her around to face him. "What is wrong with you?" His fury was tempered by genuine concern.

"I told you I'm tired, can't you just be satisfied with that?" she flung at him.

Striving to regain his temper, Logan took a deep breath. "Bryn," he began, determined to be calm and reasonable. His intension was arrested as a possible reason for her behavior became apparent. "Oh."

Anger warred with embarrassment. "Yeah, 'oh'. Damn it, damn it, damn it! I knew it! You and that…that nose of yours! Why couldn't you have just stayed away?" She turned from him, folding her arms in a defensive gesture.

"Bryn, sweetheart, you're having your period. So what? Is this what's got you all upset?" Logan felt lost. There had to more to it than this, but he just wasn't sure what.

"I was trying to spare you," she muttered resentfully.

"Spare me what?" He strove to keep the exasperation from showing.

"The smell. All that talk about how sensitive your nose is. Don't you think I smell bad?" Hurt tinged her reluctant question.

Understanding dawned. "You were worried about how I would think you *smell*?" At her nod, he was filled with compassion for the anxiety she'd needlessly suffered. He placed his hands softly on her shoulders, ignoring the tense bunching of the muscles under his hands. He gently but firmly urged her to turn around. She did, but wouldn't look at him. A steady hand under her chin raised her reluctant gaze to his. "Sweetheart, the only way you could ever smell bad to me, under *any* circumstances, is if you decided to give up bathing. And even then, I'm not sure it would matter. You do not smell bad," he earnestly reassured her. "You smell...intriguing."

A reluctant, embarrassed smile curved her lips. "Intriguing, huh? Like how? No wait, I know. It's like when a dog smells something weird in the grass and he starts rolling in it. You're not gonna roll on me, are you?" she asked with a pouting frown.

Logan chuckled, hugging her close as relief rolled over him. "I'd like to roll on you all right, but not like that."

Bryn pulled back, a look of surprise on her face. "You mean you'd make love with me?"

"In a heartbeat, baby," he stated unequivocally.

"You don't think it's...disgusting?" she asked hesitantly.

"Making love with you? Never." He deliberately misunderstood her question, hoping to rile her, to help her get her equilibrium back.

"Not that," she replied tartly. "The other, you know."

"Oh, that. No, I don't think it's disgusting. It is, and I quote, 'a natural healthy process of the female body resulting in the expulsion of a small amount of tissue and reddish fluid called blood'. Who told you it was disgusting?" he asked, correctly assuming that someone had.

"My ex-husband." Shadows filled her eyes. "I once asked him to, you know, have sex with me at that time. He said it was nasty." She hesitated, unsure about revealing any more.

"What else?" Logan prompted gently. He could tell there was more, could see her attempting to withdraw again. That idiot she had been married to was lucky he didn't live anywhere nearby. He'd done a real number on Bryn, and Logan was feeling the need for more than a little payback.

Bryn swallowed her pride and confided her shame to him. "He said it was unnatural to want to have sex when I was having my period. He said I was disgusting."

"Where does this guy live?" Logan asked with deceptive calm.

"Why?"

"I've never attacked a human while in wolf form, but for him I'm willing to make an exception." Logan's temper was stirring.

"He's not worth it." Bryn wound her arms around his neck, pulling him down for a sweet, hot kiss. "But thank you, all the same."

"You're welcome," he rumbled. "By the way, it's not unnatural. A lot of women experience heightened sexual arousal during their periods."

"So speaks the voice of experience?" she asked.

"As a matter of fact…" he began.

"Never mind, I don't want any details. How do you know about this stuff anyway?" Her curiosity was running rampant.

Logan moved to the sofa and urged Bryn onto his lap. She curled against him with a purring sigh.

He cuddled her close, stroking her hair. "One day, my very wise father sat down with my brother and me and had a little talk with us. He told us that with all the information available today, there was no reason why a man shouldn't know as much as possible about the workings of a woman's body. He said we needed to know these things, so that we could be considerate and understanding of a woman's feelings when she was experiencing these feminine functions," Logan reminisced with a grin. "Women, he pointed out, were more than penis receptacles with breasts."

"Damn right," Bryn agreed.

Logan kissed the top of her head. "He also explained to us that knowing a woman's body would make us better lovers. And that a man who was a considerate, understanding and knowledgeable lover would never lack for female companionship." Logan smiled smugly. "He was right."

"Your father sounds like a very intriguing man. Very much like his son, I imagine."

Logan acknowledged her compliment with a hug. "He's going to like you too, sweetheart. Now, are we all squared away here?"

Bryn nodded.

"Good." He stood, setting her on her feet and planting a gentle swat on her backside. "Go get your stuff, woman, we're going home."

Bryn started for her bedroom when Logan called her back. "Bring your vibrator," he ordered.

Her eyes widened in surprise as her mouth fell open. He slid a finger under her chin, gently urging it closed.

"How did you know I had a vibrator?" she asked incredulously. The surprise kept her embarrassment at bay.

He shrugged with negligent ease. "Just a hunch."

She frowned and went down the hallway to her bedroom, glancing back at him with suspicion in her eyes. Something was not quite kosher here. She was beginning to worry that he really could read her mind.

Logan smiled and waved her on. He turned on the television and settled on the couch, waiting while she packed.

Half an hour later Bryn reappeared with a suitcase. Logan made the trip to her bedroom to retrieve her makeup case and the long, zippered bag that held her work clothes. He set them on the sofa and turned to Bryn.

"Give me the vibrator," he commanded, hand extended.

"Why?" she asked, genuinely puzzled.

"You won't be needing it anymore," he assured her simply, arrogantly.

She opened her makeup case and liberated the vibrator, handing it over. Logan examined it, turning it on.

"Jealous?" she teased, as a glowing blush lit her face.

"Do I need to be?" he asked dangerously, a darkly sensual and sardonic smile curved his lips.

She felt her stomach quiver, her loins tighten and liquefy under his penetrating stare. "I guess not," she admitted. Her nipples tightened and pushed against the thin fabric of her bra and t-shirt.

Logan casually tossed the vibrator in the small trashcan by the television. "Come here." He drawled the sultry order.

A thrill shot up her spine and she smiled. "I love it when you do that," she breathed.

"What?" he inquired with a raised brow.

"Get all hot and sexy," she explained. "And then you say 'come here' in that smooth, velvety voice that makes me want to melt into a big sloppy puddle."

"Don't melt yet, baby," he countered. "Not until I've had my way with you."

* * * * *

The ride to Logan's was pleasant, thanks to their restored harmony. Bryn asked Logan to tell her about his trip and the job, which he did, with great detail.

"The whole thing seems so surreal," she said wonderingly as they arrived, exiting the car and entering the house. "You've been mediating a territory dispute between packs. Wolf packs. Wolf packs who just happen to be people, too." She shook her head. "This is going to take some getting used to."

"Does it bother you, Bryn? Knowing that we really exist?" Logan asked, flipping the switch to illuminate the stairway.

He wanted—no, *needed*—to know how she was adjusting to the shocking knowledge he'd bestowed upon her. Their relationship depended on her ability to accept his people, to accept him, fully, without reservation.

Bryn thought a moment. "You know, there's been a lot of movies and books written about werewolves. Most of them depicted werewolves as humans who changed into violent, out of control creatures. Creatures whose only goal seemed to be to kill." She paused, considering her words. "Even though there was supposedly no such creature, it was scary." She moved to stand before Logan, her eyes filled with love and acceptance. "But now, knowing you, who you are and what you can become, I'm not scared." She smiled as her hand reached up to stroke his cheek. "If you're representative of what real werewolves are like, I think we'll get along just fine."

He tipped her face up for a warm, loving kiss. "Have I told you that I love you, Bryn Roydan?" he asked softly.

"I believe you may have, a time or two," she replied, nibbling his bottom lip, "but feel free to mention it anytime you like."

"You're so good to me," he teased. "Let's go to bed."

Logan grabbed his duffel and Bryn's luggage and followed her up the stairs. "By the way, did I mention how much I like those boxers?" He admired the flexing muscles of her firm, rounded cheeks and the sexy sway of her hips as she climbed the stairs before him. "From this angle, the teddies are doing a tango."

Bryn laughed. "Stop ogling my teddy bears, you pervert."

"If I had a free hand I'd do more than ogle," he grumbled.

They reached the bedroom and Logan dumped the luggage on the bed. He and Bryn companionably unpacked their respective bags. He followed her into the bathroom, placing his toothbrush and other toiletries in their accustomed spots. While he did this, Bryn was putting her shampoo and conditioner on a shelf in the tub and putting her own things neatly on the counter. Logan noted the box of tampons she placed with her other things.

He moved behind her and, placing his hands on her shoulders, began a gentle massage. "How are you feeling, baby?" he asked solicitously.

"Fine," she replied, closing her eyes. "Mmm, that feels good."

He swept her hair over one shoulder and bared the back of her neck. Placing soft nuzzling kisses there, he slid his hands down her back and around her waist. One hand continued down over her belly to rest above her mound. "No cramps?" he asked, massaging softly.

"Uh-uh." His hands and lips had her sinking into a trance-like state.

He reached forward, tapping his finger on the box of tampons to get her attention. "Are you using one of these?" At her nod, his mouth moved to her ear. His tongue traced the fine whorls and curves. He took her earlobe into his mouth to nibble and suck. Bryn moaned as Logan stoked the tiny flame in her belly until it began to burn brightly. "Get rid of it, sweetheart," he whispered.

His firm demand sent a shiver of anticipation down her spine. Again she nodded, her eyes dreamy, her arousal rising. Logan took a towel from the cupboard and exited to the bedroom, giving her privacy. Bryn undressed and prepared herself. Slipping into Logan's robe she entered the bedroom. Logan had done a little preparing of his own. The lights had been turned out and half a dozen candles gleamed from various points in the room, casting a subtle glow.

He'd spread the towel on the bed, undressed, and now sat cross-legged, his back pressed against the headboard. Casually and comfortably nude, his erection standing full and hard, he waited for her.

"Come here." His gentle command had Bryn's insides quivering with anticipation. She discarded the robe and took the hand he offered. "I want you to sit here, in the cradle of my legs, and put your legs around my waist." He pulled her slowly, firmly toward him.

His dictate was soon accomplished with a little breathless and giggle-filled maneuvering. She settled herself in his lap, her legs spread wide and circling his muscled torso, her arms over his shoulders and around his neck. Logan folded her into his embrace, pulling their bodies firmly together. His throbbing cock rested in the open valley of her swelling sex, the plum-shaped head rubbing the satiny smooth skin of her belly.

"Oh yeah," he breathed. "You feel so good, baby."

Her breasts were flattened to his chest. The wiry hair there abraded her turgid nipples, pulling a moan from her parted lips.

Logan leaned back and slid his hands into her hair, his fingers firmly holding her as he pulled her down to his kiss. His mouth slanted over hers, rubbing and nudging to find the perfect fit. His tongue slipped out, teasing then coaxing her to open for him.

Bryn did so, willingly taking him into her mouth, suckling the tormenting invader. Logan groaned as the suctioning pull of her mouth on his tongue sped straight to his cock. They ate at each other, giving and taking, reveling in the sultry, deliberate exchange.

Logan's mouth broke from hers and began a leisurely exploration. He kissed and nibbled along her jawline to the tender hollow beneath her ear. There, he lightly pinched the vulnerable flesh between his teeth and suckled long and soft, marking her. Bryn's soft, breathy moans urged him on. Her head tilted back, exposing the long graceful column of her throat. Accepting her invitation, his mouth trailed down the silky skin. The phantom brush of his breath, warm and moist, sent each tiny quivering nerve ending dancing. At the base of her throat he paused, suckling lightly, marking her again.

"Are you giving me hickeys?" Bryn asked helplessly. Her hands feathered through his hair, holding him to her. She felt the sting as blood was suckled to the surface of her skin.

"Mmm-hmm," he purred.

"More," she demanded.

Lost in the rapture of his slow explorations and the tiny burning bites as he marked her, Bryn rocked against him. The thick column of his turgid staff slid in the fluid that leaked from her pulsing sheath. Yearning to be filled, the slow rub of his cock against her swollen clit was a torment. She struggled to rise, to impale herself.

Logan held her firmly. "Not yet sweet, not yet," he murmured in a dark, lazy drawl. "Soon baby, just hold on to me, love," he crooned at her wordless pleading whimpers.

He trailed his mouth down her chest, stopping at the slope of one firm, pale breast. He suckled fervidly, raising another passion mark on her lightly golden, silky skin. Logan's own passions were rising fast. Bryn's insistent movements and sweet, imploring moans were driving him wild. The urge to sink into her hot, clenching channel was almost overwhelming. But he had set his course, determined to see it through. A long, slow ride was his aim, his goal to prove to his mate that she was loved and desired under any and every circumstance that came along.

He bent her backward, one hand firmly planted on her back, the other cupping the taut globe of one breast. His mouth completed the journey to the engorged nipple of the other. His teeth closed gently at the base, his lips latched onto the rest, tongue laving the hardened bud as he suckled lustily.

"Logan. Ah, Logan!" Bryn cried out as a small shuddering orgasm took her. His deep growl of encouragement vibrated her sensitized flesh, sending her over another peak.

"That's good, baby, so good. I'm going to suck your other nipple now, Bryn. I want you to come for me again, baby." He quickly switched, vigorously suckling at her other nipple while his fingers tweaked and rolled the damp nub of the previous one. With a groaning cry, Bryn came again. Her body bucked against his, her sex battering his cock with each convulsive jerk of her hips.

His mouth took hers in a searing kiss, his tongue breaching all barriers, ardently exploring, savoring her unique flavor. He swallowed her pleading moans and whimpers. The scent of her arousal inundated his nasal passages as the scorching heat of her sleek, satiny skin slid against him.

Logan went into sensory overload. He was drowning in the very essence of her, of his mate. His hands cupped her buttocks, effortlessly lifting her. "Guide me in," he ordered in a thick, husky growl. She eagerly complied, directing the thick pillar of his erection to her weeping slit. When the firm, fleshy head nuzzled in, he slowly lowered her, easily breaching the taut flesh that quivered and tightened around the welcomed invader.

Bryn absorbed with single-minded fervor the impact of each solid inch of him as he slid slowly inside, filling her. Eyes closed, brow wrinkled in concentration, she rocked against him chanting, "Yes, yes, yes."

Logan gave an agonized groan as her tight passage squeezed his tunneling cock. He grunted with relief as he hilted, bottoming out against her cervix. They both stilled, holding each other, breath panting from open mouths as they reveled in the oneness of being joined.

"Ride me, Bryn," Logan commanded. Her quivering, constricting sheath was rousing him beyond measure.

Bryn's legs tightened around his waist as she began rocking, rising a short space only to sink back, feeling the gentle, rhythmic, jabbing punches of his cock head against her cervix. Wanting more, Logan grasped the taut, flexing cheeks of her bottom, lifting her. His cock pulled free, then drilled deep in a long wet slide.

"Please, please Don't stop, don't stop, don't stop!" Bryn was frantically racing to the edge.

Logan's own finish was fast approaching. He braced his back against the headboard, his hips stabbing upward, meeting each downward slide, pounding deeper. His heavy balls pulled up tight.

"Brynnn!" Her name was torn from his throat in a deep, gravel-filled groan. His throbbing cock jerked as it repeatedly spurt hot ropes of thick white cum into her already drenched passage.

Feeling the splash of his cum filling her sent Bryn barreling over the edge. Her vagina tightened and released in fluttering spasms as climax washed over her laboring body. Her wailing cry of completion rang out, the final evidence of total carnal fulfillment.

They clung to each other as individuality melted around the edges and they merged into one sensual, writhing beast.

Sweat-soaked skin slid, then stuck together as all movement gradually stilled, except the rise and fall of chests as lungs labored to replenish depleted oxygen. Night's silence reemerged. Outside, frogs and crickets sang, leaves rustled as a small breeze filtered through them. Inside, a muffled creak announced the settling of the house. The soft whir of the ceiling fan accompanied the even softer sigh of breath from two people lost in each other.

"Are you all right, sweetheart?" Logan inquired softly.

"Mmm-hmm." Her faint murmur was accompanied by several soft kisses on the shoulder where her head rested.

"As soon as I can get my knees unlocked we're going to have a shower."

Bryn tightened in his arms, attempting to disengage and rise.

"No, baby, don't move," he instructed. "Just give me a minute and I'll take care of everything."

He felt her body go limp, gratified that she put her trust in him so completely. With a groan, Logan straightened his legs and twisted to the side, swinging them down to the floor. He sat a moment, holding Bryn securely against him until his knees felt steady enough to rise. Another groan accompanied the surge to his feet and he walked to the bathroom with Bryn still wrapped around him. "I can walk," she offered.

"Just stay with me, babe. I'll get us there," he promised, each step becoming steadier with returning blood circulation.

By the time he reached the bathroom Logan was in full control again, and grabbing a washcloth, he easily stepped into the tub, standing Bryn upright. He held her pliant body against him as he adjusted the water temp and hit the shower switch. Warm steamy water cascaded over their grateful bodies.

Logan let the water soak the washcloth and lathered it up with the bar of soap kept in the shower. He began washing Bryn, running the cloth methodically over her body. Conscious of her delicate condition, he was determined to be considerate and make this just a shower and not a prelude to more sex. When he reached her belly and began moving lower she grabbed his arm. "I can do the rest," she insisted shyly.

"I want to," he replied, his steady gaze filled with love.

She bit her lip and nodded, as though afraid to speak.

Logan continued his ministrations, carefully cleansing and rinsing every part of her body. His touch was tender, gentle and very thorough. As soon as he finished, Bryn took the washcloth from him, rinsing it under the shower spray and lathering it again.

"Your turn," she smiled, and began washing him every bit as thoroughly as he had her.

She slid the soapy cloth over his arms and chest, then moved around to wash his broad shoulders and back. Logan made a growl of contentment that had her chuckling. She continued downward, soaping the tight little cheeks of his butt, sliding the cloth between them.

"Damn, baby," Logan gasped, the muscles flexing convulsively under her hands as the rough, textured cloth caressed his sensitive anal opening.

Bryn dropped the washcloth and took the soap in her hands, lathering them. She moved in front of him and ran her tongue over her bottom lip in anticipation. Just as she'd hoped, Logan's cock had begun to stiffen. Her soap-slicked hands took possession of his staff, working the turgid flesh until it was fully erect.

"What are you doing, Bryn?" he groaned.

"Taking you," she answered with succinct determination.

Bryn directed him to face the shower and rinsed him and her hands. She turned the water off and went to her knees in front of him. Her slender fingers wrapped around his throbbing length as her tongue took a long, firm swipe over his bulging cock head. Logan jerked and groaned as his breathing began to speed up.

Smiling with smug satisfaction, Bryn took his cock in her mouth, licking and sucking with unbridled enthusiasm. His hands fisted in her hair. His hips began a slow pumping motion as she worked his straining rod. Small humming sounds of pleasure made their way up her throat, vibrating his taut flesh. Logan groaned again, increasing the speed of his thrusts. He looked down and almost came at the sight of his cock, glistening with her saliva, as it slid between the full lips that she tightened around him.

Eyes closed, he was so overwhelmed with the feel of her sucking him, he didn't see or feel her take her hands away. She groped blindly for her bottle of conditioner and squirted a small amount in the palm of her left hand. Lubricating the middle finger of her right hand, she reached around behind him, spreading his flexing cheeks. The slick digit located the tight bud of his anus and slid part of the way inside.

"Ah god, baby!" he cried out.

Her left hand returned to the base of his cock, the fingers wrapping around, applying pressure as he continued to thrust into her hot, suckling mouth.

Bryn took him with pleasure. She'd never realized what an erogenous zone her mouth was. She reveled in the feel of his thick, hard cock as it filled her. She could feel the beat of his heart in the knotted veins that ran the length of him. Her tongue slid over them and over the plum-shaped head, rubbing the sensitive underside and exploring the little opening at the tip.

"I can't hold back. I'm gonna come, baby" he called out, his thigh muscles like rocks as he braced himself for the unleashing ecstasy. A guttural groan tore from his lips as she drove her finger deep into his anus. His cum spewed like lava from an exploding volcano. Bryn convulsively swallowed each thick eruption, once, twice, again and again. She withdrew her finger in a long, rapid slide. Logan groaned again as another sharp convulsive spasm tore a final burst of cum from his drained balls. His spasmodic thrusts slowed and ended. Logan sank to his knees in front of her, blissfully depleted.

He took her face in his hands, his forehead resting against hers. "Where the hell did you learn that?" he gasped.

"I read a lot," she snickered, pleased beyond measure to have given him such overwhelming pleasure.

"Thank god for books. Felt like my balls turned inside out," he quipped weakly.

Bryn reached down and lightly fondled the balls in question. "Nope, they're still right-side out," she teased. "Come on, let's finish this shower. I'm worn out."

Together they struggled to their feet and turned the shower back on, quickly rinsing down. They helped dry each other with warm, fluffy towels. Logan headed for bed as Bryn lingered over face and body lotion and the reinsertion of another tampon. Turning out the bathroom light, she stood in the doorway to the bedroom.

Logan had extinguished all the candles save one. It cast a golden glow over the bed. He lay on his back, his face and body peaceful and relaxed. A soft smile curved her lips as she studied the shadowy contours of his face. She could almost see the image of the wolf superimposed over his ruggedly handsome features. A shiver of wonder ran down her spine. He was hers. She loved and was loved in return.

Joy filled her being as she crossed the floor to the bed. Blowing out the remaining candle, she slipped under the covers, snuggling close to the heat of his firmly muscled body. A garbled murmur flowed from his lips as he tightened his arm around her, practically pulling her on top of him. She gently stroked his cheek and settled herself against him, drifting into dreams of wolves running with silent, ghostly grace under the light of a benevolent, silvery moon.

Chapter Seven

ஐ

"What's he doing here?"

Bryn had just started down the stairs when Logan admitted Reece and directed him through to the kitchen. After postponing Reece's first workout a few days ago, Logan was eager to get started. Glancing up, he spotted Bryn and instructed Reece to go on down to the basement.

"Hi, baby, you look beautiful. Come here." He met her at the bottom step and took her in his arms, kissing her with abandon.

Bryn was dressed for work in a sleek tailored blazer and skirt in a soft delicate pink with a white tank top underneath. It was the first time she'd worn this particular outfit, and studying herself in the mirror, she'd hoped Logan would approve. Obviously he did. She moaned with pleasure under his ardent assault.

Logan drew back and contemplated his mate. "I don't know how you do it," he observed. "You always look so fresh and sweet and innocent, and underneath you're a wanton, sexy little vixen."

"I don't like to show my true personality," she joked. "I'd have to fight the men off with a stick."

"Good thing," he glowered. "But you wouldn't be fighting them off. Not after I got through with them."

Bryn's eyes went wide. "Hey, we're just joking here, right?" She slid her hands through his hair, soothing and caressing. "I'm with you, Logan. I don't want anyone else."

Her gentle caress calmed him. "Sorry, baby," he apologized. "I've never been in this position before. I see you getting ready to head out the door and I just want to grab you and keep you right by my side." He steered her toward the kitchen. "Guess I'm feeling a little possessive. Just slap me down if I get too weird," he muttered.

"That is so sweet." She wrapped her arms around his neck and pressed a soft, sweet kiss to his lips. "I won't slap you." At his raised eyebrow, she hedged, "Not for that. But I will make love to you tonight." She bestowed another soft lingering kiss. "Just to show you how much I love you." Another kiss, and a teasing touch of tongue against his lips. "And to prove that you're the only man I want." Another kiss. "The only man I need."

Logan drank in her soft kisses, her warm breath against his lips, her words of love. He pulled her tight against him. "Bryn."

"Hey, Logan, do you...?" Reece had started through the basement door then paused at the sight of Logan and Bryn locked in each other's arms, "Sorry," he apologized with a sheepish look, "I'll just go back to what I was doing," he offered and retreated back to the basement.

"I'll be down in a few minutes, Reece," Logan called out after him.

"What *is* he doing here?" Bryn asked, a puzzled frown on her face.

"What with the call for the job in Montana, I forgot to tell you about his visit Sunday while you were still sleeping. Are you eating before you leave, baby?" he inquired.

"A piece of toast and a glass of milk," she replied. "Go on."

Logan got the bread and placed it in the toaster oven, while Bryn poured a small glass of milk. He explained to her about Reece's visit and how he had decided to help him.

"So you see," he continued as he buttered her toast. "If Reece can dominate Lillian, he'll be able keep her in line and out of my hair."

"Do you think she really cares about him?" she asked, taking a bite of the offered slice. She passed the toast to Logan and he took a bite. Grabbing a banana from the basket on the counter, he peeled it and handed it to her. She eyed it suspiciously. His grin at her leery expression prompted her to take a vicious bite off the end.

Logan grimaced. "Ooh, hurt me baby!"

Bryn sputtered with laughter as he took his own bite.

After chewing and swallowing he replied to her earlier question. "Yeah, I think she does care. Like I told Reece, Lillian never keeps a man around very long. The fact that she's kept him for five months is telling."

Bryn nodded her understanding. "Well, I hope you can help him. He seems like a nice guy. He's gonna need all the help he can get with *her*."

"Seems like a nice guy, huh?" Logan asked, frowning at her.

"Don't start that again," she ordered. She rinsed out her glass and, circling behind him, pinched one taut cheek.

"Hey!" he yelped, then squinted at her. "You wanna play, sweetheart?"

She held up her hand imperiously. "Stop! I have to go to work." She headed for the front door, catching up her purse and Logan's keys on the way. In the open doorway she crooked her finger at him. Sliding her free hand over his firm, muscled chest, she leaned forward, kissing him soundly. "We'll play when I get home," she promised in a sultry whisper. "Thanks for letting me borrow your car."

"Wench," Logan growled, "before you leave, I have something for you. I wanted to wait until this evening, but I can't. I want everyone to know you're mine."

He reached into his pocket and pulled out an engagement ring. White gold gleamed, framing a large diamond that glinted in the sunlight. Bryn stared at the ring with undisguised apprehension as the food in her stomach settled like a lead weight. Her gaze moved to Logan's face and she died a little inside as she watched the joy and excitement bleed from his eyes.

"I can't," she breathed. "Logan, I love you, but...I just can't. Everything's happening so fast. I need time to take it all in, time to catch my breath, to...to, I don't know," she stuttered helplessly, "to put it all in perspective."

Logan nodded, his face a stony mask, the look in his eyes, stormy. "I understand, Bryn. More than you know. But I want you to think about this. I'm not your ex-husband, or some puny, procrastinating human male who makes a promise one day and withdraws it the next. I'm an alpha," he declared proudly. "*You are my mate. Mine. My choice is not negotiable, nor will it be proven a mistake.*"

Logan turned on his heel and stalked away.

Openmouthed, Bryn stared at his retreating form. Her emotions were a roiling mass of confusion. On one hand, she felt as though she should run after him and apologize, but on the other hand, she also felt miffed at his high-handed attitude.

Breaking through her indecision, she closed the door, walked to Logan's car and settled behind the wheel. Starting the car, she headed down the driveway deciding some serious soul-searching was in order.

* * * * *

"Logan asked you to marry him, and you turned him *down*?"

Bryn cringed at the incredulous tone in Clare's voice. "I didn't turn him down. I told him I needed time to adjust to all the changes that are taking place."

Clare nodded sagely. "Yes, I can see that you'd want time for that." She gave Bryn a piercing look. "I can also see that you're afraid."

Bryn said nothing for a moment as her teeth worried her bottom lip. She hated to admit it, but Clare was right. Logan knew it, too. That was the reason he'd been so vehement that she understand he was nothing like her ex. It hurt him that she held a part of herself back through her lack of trust in him.

Assailed by guilt and shame, she lashed out. "After what happened the last time I got married, don't I have a right to be?"

"Yes, you do," Clare soothed, "but you have to remember that Logan is not your ex. When it comes to things like honesty and integrity, Logan has those in spades. Unlike someone else we both know and despise."

Bryn smiled at Clare's feeble attempt at humor.

"Do you love Logan?"

"Yes, I do. Very much."

"Then trust yourself, Bryn. Trust Logan. I think somewhere deep inside you know you can."

"I still want some time to let everything sink in. Logan's going to have to understand that I have things from my past that impact my present. I have to have time to work through them, time to deal with my fears."

"Logan's a fairly intelligent and reasonable man. I'm sure if you explain it to him, he'll understand."

Bryn laughed. "I'm sure he'd be grateful for that shining description of his finer attributes."

"Well, it doesn't do to let them know too often just how wonderful they are. They start to get bigheaded."

"Speaking of bigheaded," Bryn said slyly, "did I tell you that I don't need my vibrator anymore?"

Clare squealed with delight as they both dissolved into wicked laughter.

* * * * *

Bryn approached the house with a stomach full of butterflies. She was determined to make Logan see her point of view as far as the commitment issue was concerned, and yet she had real misgivings about the hurt and anger he had expressed at their parting this morning. What if he was every bit as determined as she? Where would that leave them?

Tears filled her eyes and she angrily blinked them away. *I'm being ridiculous*, she thought to herself as she parked the car. *We can work this out*. Despite her silent pep talk, her legs felt weak as she exited the car and walked to the door.

She took a deep breath and entered the house closing the door behind her. All was silent, and she wondered if Logan was home before his voice beckoned her from his den.

"I'm in here, Bryn."

She felt her chest tighten, her breath coming short and shallow with the anxiety she could feel building inside. Was it her imagination or did Logan's voice sound forbidding? Bryn entered the room and found Logan sitting at his desk. He stood as she entered and rounded his desk. His expression was neutral, void of its usual welcome.

Before he could reach her, she stepped back. "We need to talk," she said, feeling a twinge of foolishness and disquiet at uttering those famous and sometimes final words.

"Yes, we do," Logan agreed. He walked to the sofa inviting her to sit. She did and Logan sat on the coffee table in front of her. "Would you like to start?" he asked dispassionately.

"Yes," she breathed, and sat for a moment gathering her thoughts, her fingers twining together nervously, "I realize I hurt you this morning and I'm sorry. That wasn't my intention, but I need to make you see just how…how frightening this is for me." She bit her lip and willed the tears away, determined to stay in control. "I loved my ex-husband, Logan. I gave him all of me and he threw it away. I never knew pain like that could exist."

She looked up, her gaze meeting his. "We haven't known each other very long, but what I feel for you is *so much more*. I can't find words adequate enough to make you understand. I sometimes can't believe how much a part of me you've become." Her eyes lowered and fixed on her hands, her fingers white with the pressure of her grip. "If something happened...if you changed your mind, I couldn't...I just *couldn't.*"

Logan reached out, his hand covering the fingers that gripped each other so tightly. He felt the tension in her, sensed the fear tearing at her.

"Oh, Bryn," he murmured and pulled her trembling body onto his lap, wrapping his arms around her.

Logan rested his chin on the top of her head as he rocked her. He hadn't realized just how deeply her fears ran. He felt his hurt and anger drain away. Bryn wasn't rejecting him, she was battling her demons. He silently berated himself for putting his own selfish needs over her comfort and security.

"I'm sorry, baby. I didn't realize just how hard this is for you. I guess I'm not turning out to be such a great bargain after all," he joked softly and was surprised when Bryn's arms hugged him fiercely.

"Don't say that," she ordered, "don't even *think* it."

Logan grinned at the suddenly spirited spitfire he held in his arms. "Are you saying I might have some redeeming qualities?"

A twinkle lit her eyes and danced as a small smile curved her lips. "Maybe a few," she allowed.

Her eyes grew misty and inviting, her lips parting. Logan bent to her, gently settling his lips over hers. The kiss was long, soft and sweetly sensual. He felt the shiver that coursed through her body as she wiggled in his lap, struggling to get closer. He pulled away, smiling at her moan of frustration.

"Just one more thing," he told her as his hand cupped her breast, his fingers teasing the hardened nipple that pressed against her blouse, "then we'll take care of this. Before you left this morning you asked for time to put things in perspective. I'm willing to give you that time, within reason," he warned, "but if I'm still waiting to put a ring on your finger twenty years from now, all bets are off."

Bryn again hugged him fiercely. "Thank you, Logan, thank you, thank you, thank you." She punctuated each "thank you" with a kiss. "Now take me upstairs. I want to show you just how grateful I am."

"Faker," he accused, "you just want your own needs seen to."

"That's true," she confessed with a grin. "It's the 'two birds with one stone' effect."

Logan chuckled, rose and carried his mate upstairs where they endangered an entire flock of birds.

Chapter Eight

ॐ

The appointed day for Bryn's introduction to the pack arrived, and Bryn and Logan were making a slow drive up a long graveled road.

The road they traveled was in reality a driveway. It led to a beautiful, rustic, wood and natural rock-faced house in a large clearing, surrounded by woods. Along the way, Logan acknowledged the presence of a man stationed at the turnoff.

"He's there to keep any humans from accidentally wandering in," he explained to Bryn when she inquired. "There are others here and there through the woods keeping watch. We wouldn't want to end up on the front page of one of those gossip rags that pass for newspapers. Not that they're after us," he added, seeing her raised eyebrows. "But it doesn't hurt to be cautious."

Logan reached out, covering her hand where it lay in her lap. He squeezed gently. "Nervous?"

Bryn placed her other hand over his. "A little," she confessed. "Although not too much, now that I've met Jace and Cade and some of the others." She returned his squeeze. "Thanks to you."

Hoping to initiate Bryn slowly to the presence of other werewolves, he'd invited Jace, Cade and their dates to the house for dinner. The next week brought John Maigrey and his mate, and Dillon Bennett and his mate—an older couple who were close friends of Logan's parents.

Somewhat nervous at the beginning of both evenings, Bryn had soon settled down and enjoyed the company. Logan's friends were all very nice people, talkative, friendly, easy to get along with. The fact that they were also werewolves? Well, what the hey, she'd thought, just as with anyone else, you treat me right, I'll treat you right and we'll get along just fine. And they did.

Cars and other vehicles were parked on either side of the wide drive. Logan parked behind the last, and he and Bryn, holding hands, walked the rest of the drive and into the clearing.

"Wow, Jace really has quite a place here. It's gorgeous," Bryn commented as they walked toward the house. The house was two stories with a wraparound porch and second-floor balcony. The natural wood and stone melded and flowed with the wooded surroundings, creating an aura of belonging.

"He designed the house himself," Logan revealed. "The fact that he's an architect didn't hurt the project any."

In the grassy clearing people mingled, talking and helping themselves to soft drinks or beer from several iced tubs. Logan was hailed by more than a few people as he and Bryn neared the house. He returned their greetings and casually introduced Bryn. Many a curious glance was sent their way. Word had gotten around that Bryn was Logan's chosen, and naturally everyone was more than interested to see who had captured their pack liaison's heart.

Logan led Bryn through the crowd and up the porch steps just as Jace, Delancy, Cade and a few others came out of the house. Jace greeted Logan with a slap on the back as he bussed Bryn on the cheek under Logan's watchful eye.

"'Bout time you got here. Everybody's about to bust a gut wondering who Logan's mate is. It's all I've heard since the first bunch got here," Jace announced with some exasperation.

Logan greeted the others then replied to Jace, "Well, why don't you just settle down and make the announcement. Then you and everybody else can relax and be happy."

Jace McKenna was just as handsome in person as he'd claimed to be on the phone that day in Logan's den. Equal to Logan in height, he carried the same well-built, muscular physique. His hair, cropped stylishly short, was black as a raven's wing, his blue-green eyes filled with amber flecks.

"Well, I guess I'll do that, now that I've got permission from the all-powerful pack liaison." Jace grinned at Logan's scowl.

Jace stood silently on the porch facing the crowd, his posture straight and sure, his aura of power and command radiating outward like a wave. The chatter fell silent and all eyes turned to him.

"How did he do that?" Bryn whispered.

"That's what being an alpha is all about, Bryn," Logan replied proudly.

Sure of undivided attention, Jace began. "As you know, we've gathered here today, as we have before, to promote peace between Twin Pines and Iron Tower. And to make Logan's job a little easier." Chuckles followed Jace's announcement. "We're also here today to welcome a new addition to our numbers. Logan Sutherland has taken a mate. Greet Bryn Roydan."

Logan stepped forward with Bryn and descended the porch steps into the waiting crowd. Not sure exactly what to expect, she was nervous, but Logan's presence at her side kept her steady. The gathered crowd approached and gave quiet greeting and words of welcome. There was also, to her slight consternation, a lot of surreptitious sniffing. Nothing overt or rude, but somewhat disconcerting just the same. Some of the younger ones went so far as to take her hand and rub their cheeks against it in greeting.

"Why do they do that?" she asked Logan quietly.

"You're the mate of an alpha, Bryn, deserving of subservience from the young ones and respect from the entire pack," he explained.

The greetings continued for a few moments more before a disturbance began at the outer edges of the assembled pack. An opening was made, and through it strode Lillian Adair. A very angry Lillian. Her eyes snapped with blue fire.

"Well, isn't this just the cozy little scene," she intoned sarcastically. "Our illustrious pack liaison brings his little human twat among us and you're all panting to welcome her. Wouldn't want to miss an opportunity to kiss such influential alpha ass, now would we?"

Mutters and warning growls filtered through the crowd.

"Lillian, you go too far," Delancy warned.

"Do I, Charles?" she sneered. "As soon as I've put this human in her place, perhaps I'll put you in yours."

Gasps of disbelief rippled through the crowd. Lillian had all but challenged Twin Pines alpha. Before he could respond, Lillian faced Bryn.

"I invoke right of challenge," she declared.

"Invalid," Logan stated coldly. "Bryn's not joining Twin Pines but Iron Tower, of which you are not a member."

"I'm a member of *this*, our brotherhood and sisterhood of werewolves. Are you saying now that members of Twin Pines pack are not entitled to full rights and privileges?" Lillian asked, deliberately backing him into a corner.

"I would be the last to imply such a thing, as I'm sure you're well aware, Lillian." In his anger, Logan's eyes had bled to amber pools.

"Then my challenge stands," she stated. "Come and face me little bitch, unless you're afraid?" Her scorn was clearly apparent.

Bryn pushed forward. "I'm not afraid of you. I'm only surprised you have the guts to challenge me face-to-face. Last time you took the coward's way. I've been hoping for an opportunity for some payback."

Her words caused a stir, as everyone was well aware of the speculation that Lillian had administered the drug that had made Bryn ill.

"I'll do more than make you sick this time," she bragged, in her anger unwittingly confessing. "You're going to bleed, bitch."

Bryn, fueled with anger, started toward Lillian, "I'll show you who's the bitch, *bitch*."

Several things happened simultaneously. Logan grabbed Bryn, restraining her. Delancy and Jace came between Lillian and Bryn, and a voice rang out.

"I accept the challenge on Bryn's behalf."

Murmurs of amazement filled the stunned silence of the clearing as Reece Cofield stepped into view. It was well-known that Reece and Lillian were lovers. Bryn was the first to recover. "I don't need him to fight my battles," she declared hotly. Her blood was up and boiling hot.

"Shut her up," Jace instructed Logan.

"I can take that slut, just let me...mmmpffuc lo-aan!"

Logan wrapped a struggling Bryn securely in his arms and efficiently shut her up by the placement of one large hand over her mouth. "Unless you'd like a spanking here and now in front of all these people, you will be quiet," he ordered sternly.

Bryn gave him a mutinous glare, but subsided and stilled in his arms.

Jace turned to Lillian. "We all know that this challenge is inappropriate, Lillian. As a werewolf, even in human form your strength is far greater than that of any normal human. And although I believe Bryn—" he turned to her, giving her a wink, "—would try really hard to kick your ass, it wouldn't be a fair contest. Therefore, with Charles and Logan's approval, I believe we should let Reece stand in for Bryn."

Logan and Delancy both nodded in agreement.

Jace continued. "What will it be, Lillian? Do you withdraw your challenge or accept Reece as Bryn's champion? *Champion.* Has a nice ring to it, don't you think?"

Lillian felt her rage subsiding as hurt took its place. Reece wanted to stand in for Bryn! How could he betray her this way? After all the intimacies she'd shared with him.

Reece knew the pain she'd suffered at the loss of her mother. He knew the hurt her father's cold indifference caused her. He'd accepted and helped calm the rages that sometimes tore through her like wind through wet paper. His calm and gentle demeanor was a balm Lillian had never experienced with any other man. And now *this*, just like her father, this treachery, this *betrayal*. She felt her heart turn to ice.

"I accept her champion," Lillian stated coldly.

"Clear the area," Jace ordered. Everyone moved back, leaving an open space in which Lillian and Reece faced off.

With no hesitation or shame they began to undress. Lillian's heart pinched thinking of the times when the shedding of clothes had been a precursor to much more pleasant activities. Despite her resolve to keep him unaware of her hurt, she had to ask. "Why are you doing this?"

"I have my reasons, Lillian." Reece strove to keep his voice and expression neutral. He knew her. She kept it well hidden, but he knew he was causing her pain. His inner beast howled in anger, frustration and guilt. He kept a tight rein on himself. He knew this was their one real chance at happiness. If the only way to make Lillian see the truth was to cause her pain, than so be it. It would be well worth it, and he would soothe that pain and make her happy if he had to shove it down her throat!

"You can't win, Reece," she informed him coolly.

"Don't worry about me, Lillian. When this is done we'll both win," he assured her.

She puzzled over his reply, as she did his body as it was revealed by his disrobing. How had she failed to notice the sleek expanse of firm muscle that covered his body? He looked larger somehow, more formidable. His stance bespoke a confidence that had hitherto been lacking. Lillian felt a slight shiver of apprehension, which she quickly suppressed.

At last, standing naked, they waited.

Jace stepped forward. "Begin."

Their bodies blurred and changed in a movement so quick as to be invisible. The two wolves faced off and immediately engaged in battle.

Snarls and growls filled the air, teeth and claws fought to find purchase in the vulnerable flesh of the opponent. They charged and feinted, lunged and retreated, circling, circling, searching for the weakness that would end the contest.

The smaller she-wolf was quick and agile, she darted in and away, leaving scratches and slashes designed to slowly drain her enemy's strength. She sought to come in from behind, to hamstring her prey.

The larger male was agile enough to keep her from doing any serious damage. He knew her tactics well and kept her in front of him. His strategy was to overpower with sheer strength and drive her into submission. Her throat was his objective, not to rip and tear, but to control.

Minutes passed as the contest wore on. Lillian began to realize that she was up against a formidable opponent. Reece was blocking her every move with ease, countering her again and again. This was not the easy contest she had thought it would be and she was nearing the end of her strength. Reece had changed. Somehow, someway, he had acquired the physical ability and determination to take her down. Rage and pain warred for supremacy inside. She struggled to keep her emotions in check, knowing they would only hinder, not help.

Lillian knew that she had already lost Reece — his betrayal was unforgivable. If she lost this battle she would also lose her place, her beta status in the pack. At that moment she spotted Bryn across the clearing. It was all that *human's* fault. The pain and anger burst free, and with a tortured howl Lillian propelled herself across the clearing.

Bryn's eyes widened with fear as the maddened she-wolf bore down on her. Logan stepped in front of her, prepared to protect her at any cost. The she-wolf launched herself at her target but never made contact.

Reece too, had been prepared. He caught Lillian broadside, knocking her to the ground, hearing her breath explode from her lungs. Giving her no time to recover, he stood over her heaving, supine body and took the skin of her throat in his teeth, uttering a warning growl.

The she-wolf lay stunned, chest heaving as she fought to recover her breath. The male was over her, his teeth holding her in this hated submissive posture. She struggled weakly and was quickly subdued by a greater pressure on her throat and another, sterner growl of warning. She'd never felt so shamed, so humiliated, so humbled, so…so horny! The hot, musky smell of him was filling her senses, making her tremble, making her want to rise and present herself to him for the mating. He'd proven himself a worthy adversary, a worthy mate.

She whimpered her submission, her need. Her throat was cautiously released, a rolling growl holding her immobile. The male caught her gaze and she lowered her head in an unmistakable gesture.

Their forms shimmered and changed. Reece stood victorious over Lillian, waiting.

She looked up at him, tears shimmering in her eyes. "Why did you do this? For her?"

Reece bent down to her. "Not for Bryn, Lillian. For you. For us. I fought for *us*, baby. I love you." He reached a hand down to her.

Lillian stared at his hand and then into the eyes of the only man she had ever trusted and loved, who loved her in return, without conditions, without reservations. She placed her hand in his. "Reece." Her choked invocation of his name galvanized him into action. He pulled her up and over his shoulder in a smooth graceful move. Without a word he marched off into the woods to claim his mate.

The silence that had filled the clearing was broken by one strident voice. "Well, I'll be damned," Jace declared.

Laughter and the renewed buzz of conversation filled the air. This was an event that would be talked of for some time to come.

"You know, Logan," Jace theorized, staring in the direction of Reece and Lillian's departing forms, "that boy exhibited some moves that were awfully familiar looking." He turned, pinning Logan with a thoughtful stare. "You wouldn't know anything about that, would you?"

"Not a thing," Logan answered easily, his face a study in innocence.

Delancy looked from Jace to Logan and shrugged. "Looks like Twin Pines has a new beta. It sure will be nice having Lillian off my back." He wandered away with a satisfied smirk.

Jace snorted in disgust, a sneer twisting his lips. "Dumbass doesn't even realize his troubles have just begun. Five'll get you ten, next year, Reece is Twin Pines alpha," he offered.

Logan upped the stakes. "Six months, tops. Make it twenty and you got yourself a bet."

Jace considered for a moment then stuck out his hand. "Done."

"Done," Logan repeated as they shook on it.

Jace took a still pouting Bryn's hand in his. "By the way, in all the excitement I almost forgot. Welcome to the pack."

"Thanks." Bryn made a sulky moue. "I still say I could have taken her."

Logan gave her a healthy swat on the ass, then soothingly rubbed her abused flesh. "Bloodthirsty vixen, settle down. Show a little respect for your alpha."

"Which one?" she groused.

"Both," Logan and Jace answered simultaneously, and laughed at her grimace of annoyance.

The atmosphere noticeably lightened as the packs dispersed into smaller groups to discuss the fight. It seemed Logan and Jace were not the only ones predicting the rise of a new alpha for Twin Pines pack. Many a speculative glance was sent toward the unsuspecting Delancy.

Bryn found John Maigrey and his mate, Becca, stopping to talk with them as Logan and Jace wandered away, intent on a discussion involving boundary etiquette. After the confrontation with Lillian, she was content to relax in the company of the older couple, at first unaware of the sexual undercurrents sparked by the fight.

Her tranquility was short-lived.

With her back to the majority of the group, she paused mid-sentence as a wave of unease passed over her. Bryn turned around to discover that Logan was surrounded by at least a dozen women. All of them were touching him in some manner, the sensual slide of a hand down his back, chest or arms, the deliberate brush of a curved body against his.

As though taking a blow to the solar plexus, Bryn felt an immediate shock of pain. Logan was doing nothing to discourage them! Not only that, he seemed to be *enjoying* their attention.

One by one, the women began to shed their clothes. Logan turned his gaze to Bryn, his eyes beginning to shine with that familiar molten-gold color that told of his arousal. His expression conveyed a question. And a challenge.

Bryn began to see red as the pain dissipated, anger taking its place. "What the *hell* is going on?" she growled.

Jace, who had silently made his way to her side, spoke softly in her ear, "They choose to ignore your claim. They're presenting themselves for Logan's pleasure. Although he wears your scent, unlike you, he's unmarked."

"Unmarked?"

Jace gently touched the tiny marks that had been left behind when Logan bit her during their lovemaking. "These marks," he explained.

Fire flared in her eyes as she glared at the scene unfolding before her eyes. "Marks or no, he's mine," she hissed, and began stalking toward the group that circled Logan.

Unbeknownst to her, Jace wore a smile of satisfaction as he watched her prepare to claim her mate.

Held in the thrall of an instinct so primal and basic that it couldn't be stopped, couldn't be questioned, Bryn was ready to fight for what was hers.

Her steely gaze locked with Logan's as she moved toward him. Sparks flared in his golden eyes, kindled by the sensual deliberation of her approach. Bryn ignored the women surrounding him, passing through their midst as though they were invisible.

One boldly stepped directly into her path.

Without a word, Bryn stared at the interloper, her gaze hard, determined and unwavering. The would-be poacher at first returned her regard, but finally, intimidated by Bryn's unswerving resolve, she lowered her eyes and stepped away.

Bryn continued forward until she faced Logan. "In case you've forgotten, *you're mine*," she declared.

"As you're mine," Logan agreed.

Captured by irresistible impulse, Bryn threw herself into Logan's arms and wrapped her legs around him. A feral growl left her throat as she felt his erection press into the apex of her jean-clad thighs. She ground herself against him, gasping with pleasure as his hands grasped and kneaded the firm mounds of her rounded bottom.

Oblivious to the watchers that gathered around them, Bryn captured Logan's lips, her tongue ravishing the warm, welcoming cavity of his mouth. She swallowed the rumbling groan that he uttered, feeling the vibration in her heavy, swollen breasts, where they pressed firmly against his chest. Without shame, she pressed her body into his, wanting nothing more at that moment than to be joined with him, to back up her claim with a mating.

She released his mouth, her lips moving over the hard ridge of his jaw and down the sensitive skin of his neck to his shoulder. She pushed his shirt aside and laved his warm, golden skin with her tongue, pulling another moan from Logan. A wicked, satisfied smile ghosted across her lips a split second before she set her teeth to his shoulder and bit.

Logan threw his head back, the sound issuing from his throat a near howl. Bryn felt their bodies descend as Logan's knees buckled with the pleasurable pain of her bite. She kept her grip and found herself on his lap, her legs still wrapped tightly around his body. Mindlessly, she bucked against the thick bulge of his cock.

With a savage growl, Logan rolled and brought her beneath him, thrusting himself against her with a hard steady rhythm. His hands found the open collar of her shirt and yanked, sending the buttons flying, revealing the delicate lace of her bra. Pushing one cup down, his mouth fastened on her engorged, sensitized nipple. Bryn cried out, her back arching as he suckled her.

Inflamed by their mutual need, climax exploded between them. Logan's guttural groan joined Bryn's wail as their bodies writhed in completion.

Bryn lay in a sated heap, Logan's body draped over hers, as small aftershocks pulsed through her. Eyes closed, she could feel the hard rhythm of their hearts ease, just as their breathing slowed to normal. She'd momentarily forgotten just where they were until a voice pierced the pleasurable fog that filled her brain.

"I'd say you're now officially mated."

Bryn gasped and froze. "Oh. My. God," she whispered. "Look what you made me do!"

Logan snorted with amusement. "I made you do this? You practically raped me, Bryn."

"Well, I wouldn't have, if you hadn't been ogling those other women."

"I didn't initiate that, and I wasn't *ogling*."

"You were practically drooling!"

"I was not!"

"You were so!"

Jace squatted down next to them. "Children, let's not squabble," he told them reasonably, before looking up at the gathered pack members. "No mistake about it, they're *definitely* mated." He winked at the two of them and rose to saunter away amidst the laughter of the dispersing pack.

Bryn and Logan looked at each other and grinned.

"Come on." Logan stood and offered his hand to Bryn.

She adjusted her bra and pulled her shirt together, all the while studying him. Putting her hand in his, she let him help her up.

"Let's go home," he said.

He put his arm around Bryn's shoulders and led her back in the direction of the car. Bryn began to giggle.

"What's so funny?"

"That's a nice wet spot you've got on the front of your jeans."

"Don't push it, girlie," he warned.

Bryn just smiled and kept walking.

* * * * *

Later, in the early morning hours, Logan awoke with a raging hard-on and the fertile scent of Bryn bewitching his soul. Mate—mate in *heat*. The scent was so pure and alluring, so rich, ripe and mesmerizing, he was compelled, without conscious thought, into action.

He rolled her pliant body to her stomach and pulled her to her knees, stuffing pillows under her. Spreading her thighs and holding her firmly, his mouth and tongue found her pussy. Her spellbinding scent filled his nostrils, adamantly demanding his attention. A few laps at her slit as he pierced her with his tongue, along with small sucklings of her clit had copious cream flowing. Before she was fully awake he had her aroused and mounted.

Bryn came awake, a moan flowing from her throat as Logan slid fully inside her suddenly pulsing sheath, burying himself to the hilt. He lay over her, unmoving except for the short jabbing thrusts of his hips against her lush bottom that sent the plump head of his cock knocking at her womb.

"It's time," he groaned. "God baby, you smell so *gooood*." His husky growl sent her vagina into clenching spasms, massaging his buried shaft.

"Mmm, Logan. Baby, please. More. More!" Bryn struggled under him, pushing back, taking more of the thick column that filled her. Her body tightened, quivering and shuddering, joyously beginning the journey into ecstasy.

Logan obliged and rose over her. Grasping her hips in an almost bruising grip, he alternated long gliding thrusts, with short rapid-fire digs, igniting every nerve ending in

Bryn's sensitized core. He mated her in a fast frenzied rush that left her gasping for breath.

The bed rocked and shuddered under their writhing bodies. Grunts, moans, labored breaths and gasps of pleasure joined the night's serenade, while the rich ambrosial aroma of their joined bodies flavored the air.

A hand at her shoulder and an arm around her waist pulled her upright to her knees, held tight to the hard, corded muscles of his chest. Still fully impaled on his thick shaft, she felt the insistent throb of it buried in her depths. Bryn moaned, squirming in protest at the cessation of movement.

"Shh. Hush, baby, take a minute. Just a minute." Logan's breath, warm and moist, gusted in her ear. "Ahhh, Bryn, you're so tight around me, baby, so good, so good," he praised.

Bryn whimpered and twisted in his arms, desperate to complete the journey. His hand slid from one shoulder to the other as he looped his arm across her chest. His other hand covered her belly. Expertly stilling her struggles, he held her to him, their sweat-slicked skin sliding together with wanton friction. "Listen to me, Bryn, listen to me." He waited as she stilled, her breathing slowed, a convulsive shudder vibrating the length of her spine where it pressed against him. "You're ovulating, baby. If I come inside you, you'll get pregnant. Do you want my child, Bryn? Do you want to become one with the pack?"

As lost as she was in the passionate joining of their bodies, she still felt the magic of the moment at hand, of the results this wild ride would bring. "Our child, Logan," she panted. "Yes, I want our child, I want the pack, I want you." Tears rolled down her cheeks. Her head fell back against his shoulder. "I told you, *I told you*." Her breath shuddered as her chest tightened with emotion.

"It's all right, baby, it's all right," he crooned. Logan felt his emotions take flight. Visions of running with her in wolf shape, of Bryn carrying their child, the wonder of knowing he would soon have a son or daughter. He felt his own chest constrict with joy. A sheen of tears enhanced the golden glow of his eyes as he swallowed hard to contain them.

Passion reasserted itself, impatience rode her hard. "No, it's not all right," Bryn declared hotly. "If you don't stop fucking around and start fucking *me*, I'm going to kill you!" She bent forward and sank her teeth into the forearm draped across her chest.

"Son of a bitch!" Logan yelled, then laughed, which dragged a simultaneous groan out of their throats as his shaft rocked inside her clasping channel. Her tongue slid over the indentations of the mark she'd left behind in his flesh. Her unexpected attack sent a wild streak of arousal coursing through his veins. His cock pounded with a fresh influx of blood, which made him thicken and swell to an almost painful degree. With a deep growl, he bent her forward, forcing her down, holding her in the submissive position for his renewed thrusts.

Waves of primitive, feral impulse washed through her. She struggled, returning his growl with one of her own, snarling at her mate, wanting him, yet needing to fight, needing to test his strength, his worthiness to have her, to father their children. Fierce, bestial aggression had her twisting against him and fighting his possession.

Logan's own inner savage surfaced. It gloried in the contest. His will strong, his purpose sure, he dominated his mate, demanding her submission. He easily countered every willful test of his authority. He allowed her to battle his dominance, giving her proof of his fitness to rule her.

Finally his indulgence was pushed to the breaking point. He blanketed her body, controlling her. "Enough!" he ground out roughly. The power of the wolf shimmered through him. Logan felt the slight lengthening of his jaw, his incisors growing long and sharp. Finding the vulnerable curve between neck and shoulder that held his mark, he bit down, breaking the skin and tasting the sweet, hot, metallic spice of her blood.

Bryn stilled and whimpered at the pain that, in a blinding flash, became pleasure as he held her for his deep hard thrusts. Again and again he drove into her, his teeth subduing her. There were no more thoughts of dominance and submission, only the wild surges of pleasure that took them both.

A tremor shook her body as a wave of wildfire swept through her veins. Thrust into a conflagration of heat so intense she would afterward swear her skin had melted, she was held anchored only by the sharp sting of Logan's bite and the repeated invasion of his pounding cock. Bryn bucked and writhed under him as her temperature spiked, unaware that Logan had begun to come until she felt the first molten jet of seed drench her already inundated passage. Distantly she heard his guttural growl of release, his muffled curse. Her mind barely registered what her body welcomed until she felt him swell, felt the hard knot form in the thick column of his cock as he strove to continue thrusting. She pushed back desperately, instinctively helping him to bury himself to the root. Her pliant sheath expanded, then molded the distended pulsing flesh that invaded her, locking in a vise-like grip as her orgasm detonated and she rode the licking, crackling flames until she felt her body drift like ash to land with a soft whisper on the waiting sheets.

Barely given time to recover, she felt another hard pulse of Logan's buried shaft, which caused it to nudge her cervix. Bryn moaned and quivered as another orgasm tightened her inner flesh around him. Her shudders eased and she became aware of Logan, draped over her, his chest rising and falling in concert with her own slowing breaths. He'd rolled their bodies slightly to the side so that she wasn't crushed beneath him. Instead, she lay partially on the pillows he had stuffed under her, sandwiched between their cushiony softness and the firm, enveloping heat of Logan's body. His cock had taken on truly massive proportions, remaining fully engorged. Rapid throbbing emulated a vibrator as it pulsed against the velvety enclosure of her sheath.

Logan lay against Bryn, eyes closed, waiting for the next spasmodic jerk of his cock that would release more of his seed to his mate's waiting womb. It was like riding an agonizingly long, slow wave of pleasure until it suddenly peaked, cresting, then sliding down to again ride the wave, waiting for the next peak.

He hadn't believed his father when he'd explained the phenomenon to his brother Dylan and him. How his mate's temperature would rise and peak in a blaze of heat so intense it would trigger the canine-like knot that would form in his penis, locking them together, ensuring his seed would take root. But here he lay, trapped inside the slick grasping berth of Bryn's sheath, waiting for the next pulse, the next jet of cum. Logan smiled. *Wait 'til I tell Dylan*, he thought. *The old man wasn't bullshitting us*. His smile turned to a grimace as the next peak hit. His balls drew up, releasing another load of creamy, potent semen.

"Ah shit, shit," he murmured as he rode the wave.

Bryn's back arched as another orgasm struck. Her short desperate whimpers were muffled against the pillow.

"That's it, baby," Logan groaned. "Bryn, ah god, Bryn," he gasped as she tightened around him.

They lay quiet as the spasm eased, sucking in needed oxygen for laboring lungs. As her breathing steadied, Bryn stirred.

"Did you know this was going to happen?" she asked, her body still quivering with the aftershocks.

"Dad mentioned it," Logan gritted out. "I thought he was kidding."

"Hmm," she acknowledged. The endless throbbing vibrations set her nerves dancing. She shivered. "How long does it last?"

"According to Dad, 'bout a half hour or so," Logan replied, his hands absently caressing her soft moist skin. "Why? You bored?"

"Hardly," she scoffed.

As predicted, a half hour later a final wrenching pulse hit. Bryn's body bowed as Logan's hips gave one convulsive, heaving thrust. They both cried out as the final molten jet of seed splashed her inner walls. Collapsing with exhaustion, they felt the hard knot in Logan's cock loosen as the unyielding stiffness eased. Bryn's vagina relaxed, surrendering its stranglehold on Logan's weary flesh. He slid free, and they both sighed with relief.

Bryn weakly pushed the pillows aside and rolled to her back. "I *better* be pregnant," she warned him, although her enfeebled voice lacked any real threat.

Logan's hand covered her belly as he inhaled deeply. "He or she's in there, baby," he assured her. "Trust me." The change in her scent was unmistakable. Bryn had conceived.

She chuckled weakly and immediately drifted to sleep. Logan gathered enough strength to pull a sheet over them and without hesitation, followed her.

* * * * *

They slept peacefully for several hours until Bryn awoke with a start. She felt a strange combination of stretching and contracting aches in her limbs and throughout her body. It wasn't painful, just disorienting and confusing.

Even though the room was dark, she could see everything clearly, and when she took a deep breath to steady her nerves, her olfactory sense was inundated with data. First and foremost, Logan's scent filled her, easing her fear, calming her with his presence. She savored the smell of their bodies and the warm, musky aftermath of sex. Their mingled juices were a potent combination. Another breath brought the scent of leather and chocolate. Her purse, which lay on the wing chair across the room, and the candy bar she'd tucked inside to snack on while at work. Through the open window, the breeze swept in the scents and sounds of the night. Water, the smell sharp and tangy where it lay as dew blanketing the grass. The gurgling splash of it as it flowed from the fountain into the pool. Wind, creating diverse sounds as it flowed in endless waves. The soft rustle of the leaves on the trees, the light tapping of the branches of a bush against the house, the hushed whisper of the grass as it swayed in the garden. *Animal* — her interest peaked as she smelled the rabbit. She froze, as her muscles seemed to bunch and gather, preparing for the chase. Her mouth watered and hunger pinched her belly at the thought of fresh, warm, bloody meat. A rumbling growl slid from her throat and she started with surprise.

"What the *hell*," she murmured. "Logan, wake up!" she spoke aloud, shaking him.

Totally unnecessary. He'd woken at the sound of her growl, instantly alert, his senses scanning for the threat. Finding none, he gave his attention to Bryn and relaxed, a wry smile curving his lips. Her eyes had gone molten silver. The conversion was kicking in, taking her in hand, changing her, making her werewolf.

He reached out and smoothed her hair back, tucking a strand behind her ear. "Take it easy, Bryn, it's the conversion."

"Take it easy? Are you nuts?" she yelped, incredulity and lack of sleep making her cranky. "I just sat here and contemplated catching and eating a bunny rabbit. Raw. And it sounded good. The same bunny rabbit I can hear and smell out on the lawn. Take it easy? I don't think so, buster."

Logan threw an arm around her shoulders and wrestled her back down to the bed, pulling her over his chest. "We could go out hunting if you like," he teased, knowing her refusal would be vehement and quick. He wasn't disappointed.

"Hell, no!" she vociferated, "I'm not hunting down some cute cuddly little bunny and making a meal of him."

Logan chuckled, then sobered. "You will, you know, eventually," he told her seriously. "You're becoming a werewolf, Bryn. In wolf form it will seem right and natural, and even necessary at times. The wolf requires nurturing, just as the human does. As a human you have hobbies and provide yourself with things that stimulate and entertain. These are things the wolf needs, too. Wolves have very basic joys, running with the pack, playing—" he slid a warm hand over her naked back and down to the curve of her buttock, squeezing softly, "—mating and hunting."

Bryn sighed, relaxing against him. "Don't worry about it," he soothed, yawning. "We'll have you eating raw bunnies in no time."

"Eeewww," she mumbled, as sleep took her again.

Chapter Nine

ജ

Bryn watched Logan through the open kitchen doorway. He sat on a stone bench by the koi pond, feeding the fish. A gentle breeze stirred his hair causing the red-gold glints to sparkle and dance.

Under his shirt, the muscles in his arms and shoulders bunched and moved. A small smile teased her lips—it still amazed her that such an extraordinary man could be hers.

Everything seemed perfect except for one discordant note, the engagement. True to his word, Logan had not brought the subject up again, but Bryn had a feeling it was very much on his mind. There were times when he withdrew into silence. When she asked if something was bothering him, he immediately denied it. Even though he wouldn't admit it, Bryn knew he was still troubled by her reluctance, especially now that there was surely a little one on the way.

Bryn's hand covered her still flat abdomen, an unconscious gesture of protection. Her gaze again caressed Logan, her eyes filling with love and admiration. With him she found peace and security. *Her life felt complete.* The realization flooded her with warmth and broke through her doubts, leaving behind a calm determination.

She walked slowly out of the house and across the lawn. Stopping behind Logan, she placed her hands on his shoulders, her fingers gently kneading the firm muscles.

"Mmm, that feels good, babe," he rumbled, turning his head to look up at her.

Bryn felt her heart skip a beat at the love that shone so plainly in his eyes for her. She leaned down, her lips softly meeting his. Logan twisted his body and Bryn found herself on his lap. The gentle kiss ended and Bryn looked deeply into Logan's eyes, her hand coming up to lightly brush the hair back from his beloved face.

"Logan," she said softly. "Will you marry me?"

Logan's eyes widened then crinkled at the corners as a smile slowly curved his lips. "Are you sure?"

"I'm sure."

"You know wolves mate for life, don't you?" he asked with a twinkle in his eyes.

"I wouldn't have it any other way."

Bryn breathed a soft, murmuring sigh as Logan's lips found hers in a sweet, tender kiss.

* * * * *

"How did it go?" Logan stepped into the doorway of the den and studied Bryn with a little concern. She had just called her parents to break the news about their engagement.

She smiled a little wanly. "About like I thought. They're cautiously happy."

Logan ambled in and stepped behind the desk chair where Bryn was seated. He began to massage the tightened muscles of her shoulders.

Bryn had predicted their reaction when she and Logan had decided to call their parents and begin spreading the happy news of their engagement. She knew her parents would worry after all she'd been through with her first husband. In a way, Bryn felt she'd failed *them* when her marriage had broken up.

Logan's parents had been ecstatic. The sure, unmistakable method by which a werewolf chose his or her mate had of course left them no doubt that their son had made the right choice. Bryn was a bit envious of the easy time Logan had breaking the news to his parents.

"Mmm," she hummed in appreciation as his hands firmly kneaded her taut shoulders. "They said to tell you they're looking forward to meeting you," she informed him.

He cocked a cynical brow. "I'm sure."

"They are," she assured him. "Or they soon will be, after they get the call from Clare."

"What's Clare got to do with it?" he asked with a puzzled frown.

"Mom and Dad love Clare. They trust her judgment implicitly," Bryn explained. "When she gets through giving you her glowing recommendation, it'll put their minds at ease."

Logan slowly spun her chair around to face him. He tucked a finger under her chin and forced her eyes up to meet his. "You're hurt that they trust Clare's judgment and not your own," he prodded gently.

She nodded, rising from the chair and walking to the window. "I know I made a mistake, but I..." The bleak tone of her voice made him ache for her.

"You loved him," Logan stated honestly, openly acknowledging the unpalatable fact. He followed her to the window and wrapped his arms around her, pulling her back against his chest. "I've faced the fact that you once loved another man. And I'm honestly sorry that you were so hurt by that horse's ass."

A small breathy snort of air issued from Bryn.

"But I've never been more grateful for anything in my life that he didn't make you happy." His arms tightened around her. "If he had, we'd never have met. Or if we had met, I'd have spent the rest of my life in misery, knowing that my mate belonged to another man.

"No one chooses to love, love makes the choice. Your parents know that, Bryn. I think you underestimate their understanding. They love you, and I'm sure they trust you every bit as much as they always did." He gave her an admonishing squeeze. "Let it go, sweetheart, don't make yourself unhappy for no reason."

She turned in his arms and hugged him with such fierce gratitude, he grunted with the pressure she applied. "I'd have gladly suffered ten times the pain if I'd known you'd be waiting for me at the end of it. *I love you.*" The last was squeezed out in a whisper as she fought the tears that flooded her eyes and tightened her throat.

His forehead met hers with a gentle thump. "That means everything to me, Bryn, because I trust your judgment. Implicitly."

Her watery grin touched his heart and then her sweetly sensual lips touched his, bestowing a kiss of such delicate beauty that it conveyed without words the depth of her love for him. Logan felt tears mist his own eyes as they clung together, enveloped in the warmth of their bodies and the harmonious beating of their hearts.

"By the way," Bryn murmured softly, "did I tell you my sister's coming?"

Logan groaned.

"You'll love her," Bryn promised, a teasing smile curving her lips, as a look of beguiling innocence filled her eyes. "Trust me."

* * * * *

That evening, Bryn and Logan retired to the den, where Logan lit a fire in the fireplace. August was winding down into September, and the nights had begun to turn cooler.

They lazed comfortably on the sofa, cuddled together, gazing into the fire. "Take your clothes off," Logan whispered in her ear.

"I will if you will," she replied, with a sultry smile.

"Not this time, sweetheart," Logan refused. "I'm not the one who's about to go wolfie."

Bryn's heart sped as she sat up abruptly. "Are you sure we should do this? I'm not sure I'm ready." Her hand moved protectively over her middle. "It won't hurt the baby, will it?"

Logan stood up and pulled her to her feet. "It won't hurt the cub," he assured her gently, as he began steadily unbuttoning her shirt. "You'll love it, Bryn. Believe me, it'll be easy."

Taking him at his word, she began helping him and soon stood nude, shadows cast by the firelight flickering over the light golden tint of her skin. Bryn stood, outwardly relaxed, under the growing heat in his eyes. His golden eyes began to glow, and if she had seen her own reflection, she would've noted that hers, too, shone with a silvery gleam.

Bryn noted with pleasure the growing bulge in Logan's jeans. Her tongue ran over her lower lip with sensual anticipation.

Stepping forward, Logan, showing great restraint, placed his hands on her shoulders. "Look into my eyes," he instructed her.

Bryn giggled. Seeing his frown of disapproval, she sobered. "Sorry," she apologized. "It's just that you sounded like those old vampire movies on the late show."

"Yes, I know. Now concentrate," he said with mock severity, as his lips twitched with a suppressed smile.

Bryn squelched her own smile and stared into Logan's eyes. An immediate connection was made, and she could see in her mind's eye Logan as a wolf, running with joyous abandon through the cool, leafy expanse of an endless wood. She needed to be with him. The desire was so strong and so piercing she burned with it. Heat enveloped her body and she felt a strange flowing shift that made her slightly dizzy.

As the world righted itself, she found herself staring at Logan's knees. She stepped back, confused, only to discover her two legs had become four. They worked perfectly, but the strangeness of it had her trying to check them out, which caused her body to turn in circles as she bounced around, trying to get a look at the new equipment.

Logan's laughter rang out and Bryn stilled, her wolfie dignity very much offended at his show of merriment at her display. She sat, the perfect picture of piqued majesty.

He squatted down and offered a very sincere apology. Bryn regarded him quietly for a moment, then moved forward to lick his cheek to show her acceptance. With mischievous intent, she reared up, placing her front paws on his shoulders, deliberately knocking him over. Logan rolled, laughing as she stood over him, tickling as she licked his face and neck.

Changing back with ease, she lay over him and laughed. "That was fun!" she enthused.

Logan rolled, pinning her under him with a grin. "Fun, huh? Let me show you some real fun."

Without hesitation, his mouth latched onto the firm tip of her breast and began to suckle with vigor. Bryn moaned, grabbing his head with both hands as she arched under him.

His mouth moved to her other breast, giving it a similar treatment. "Is this fun?" he questioned softly, lapping at her distended nipple.

"Oh, oh yeah," she panted. "More fun, Logan," she demanded.

Logan eased himself off of her and came to his feet, peeling his clothes off with slow deliberation. His eyes stayed with Bryn, following the curves of her delicious body, pausing here and there at the more mouthwatering parts. He lingered at her breasts, the nipples ruby red and shining with his saliva. His gaze arrowed down to her pussy, visible between her shapely parted thighs. Her mound was rounded, the outer lips puffy, moisture shining between them as her need increased.

He reached out, offering his hand. She took it and he pulled her to her feet, backing to the sofa. Seating himself, he pulled her forward and—without words—indicated she should straddle his lap. Bryn obeyed and he took his erection in hand and teased her with it.

Bryn panted and moaned as the plump, throbbing head of Logan's cock slid through the thick juice of her arousal. He repeatedly rubbed her swollen clit, then glided through her slit to her waiting vaginal entrance, applying pressure, entering a few teasing centimeters only to draw back to again taunt the needy nub of her clit.

Bryn became frantic to impale herself on his hard cock, but Logan controlled her easily as he murmured soft, crooning words of encouragement. Satisfied that she was riding the edge of orgasm, Logan again breached just the inner edge of her channel.

"Look at me, baby," he ordered. "I want to see you come."

Bryn's eyes locked with his as he slowly allowed her to lower herself, engulfing the thick, throbbing length of his cock. Her breath heaved through laboring lungs and small whimpers tore from her throat as her body tightened, tightened, tightened, then exploded. She threw her head back and wailed her release, rapidly pumping her hips against the shaft that was buried balls-deep inside.

Logan held her shuddering, quivering body as it bowed back, gritting his teeth and holding back his own release. As Bryn came back to earth he pulled her close, her head resting on his shoulder. When her breathing had evened out he eased back and she lifted her head, meeting his tender gaze. "Was that fun?" he asked, with a smug satisfied smile.

"Oh yeah," she smiled.

"Ready for more?" he questioned, as his hips pumped upward, driving his impatiently throbbing cock deeper into her hot, slick depths.

Bryn gasped, then reciprocated with a move that brought a groan from Logan. "Always," she assured him, with a smug smile of her own.

They began to move in concert, Bryn undulating against him, each movement rubbing her clit with slick friction against his pumping shaft.

Logan's hands were filled with the firm globes of her buttocks as he encouraged her movements. He kneaded the flexing mounds under his hands as he rhythmically thrust up into her clasping sheath. Her vagina tightened around him. His cock felt huge as it swelled and hardened to a final degree, preparing for ejaculation.

Feeling the tingle of eminent release at the base of his spine, he released one rounded cheek and reached between them. His fingertips found the engorged pearl of her clit. Sliding in the moisture surrounding it, they gently massaged.

"Oh, oh, oh god, Logan!" she cried, as climax again took her willing body.

Thrusting through the vise-like clasp of her slick, heated flesh, Logan burst, bathing her inner walls with the creamy warmth of his cum. He groaned as his cock jerked with each forceful jet of seed.

Totally satiated, all movement stilled as they melted together, a relaxed and loose tangle of bodies and limbs.

"Definitely fun," Bryn murmured.

Logan gave a soft snort of laughter. With a groan he rose and set Bryn on her feet. They stood together, swaying unsteadily.

"Are you going to get dressed?" he asked her.

"Nope," she answered succinctly, bending down to gather assorted pieces of clothing in her arms. Walking away with an uncoordinated wobble, Bryn stopped and looked back. "Are you coming?"

"Not yet," he leered, his eyes trained on the luscious mounds of her backside. "But keep walking, babe. I'll be ready again by the time we get upstairs."

"Ass," she commented, giving him a level stare. She turned away and continued out of the room. Secretly pleased by her effect on him, a satisfied smile curved her lips.

Logan grinned. "Exactly," he murmured, his gaze following the hypnotic movements of her bottom. He eagerly followed her up the stairs.

* * * * *

A couple of days later, Bryn's sister Hayley arrived. She took a plane as far as Hibbing and insisted on renting a car and driving herself the rest of the way to Whispering Springs.

"She's very independent," Bryn revealed to Logan, as she tried to explain Hayley's refusal to let them pick her up at the airport.

"Personally, I think she just wants to have a vehicle handy so she can make a quick getaway," Logan theorized with a smile.

Hayley arrived late in the afternoon. Bryn sprinted out of the house to meet her and they squealed with delight, hugging each other warmly. They hadn't seen each other since the traditional family Christmas gathering at their parents' home eight months earlier, and had a lot of catching up to do.

Logan lounged in the doorway, giving them privacy, studying Bryn's sister curiously. The resemblance was unmistakable.

Bryn looked around for Logan and motioned him to them. Hayley studied Logan in turn and found him to be all Bryn had described. It seemed her sister had really hit the jackpot. Logan was a hunk, Hayley thought with a frisson of envy. She mentally chastised herself as she looked at Bryn. Her sister's face shone with happiness as she watched Logan's approach. Anyone who could heal the wounds that Jeffrey-the-asshole had inflicted on her beloved sister was worthy of her respect and affection. Hayley was determined not to be jealous of her sister's good fortune. Even though her own relationship had just ended up in the crapper.

Bryn introduced them and they exchanged polite greetings. "Bryn didn't exaggerate," Hayley began after shaking Logan's hand, "you *are* a big man."

Logan stilled, at a loss, not sure how to respond to her comment.

Hayley's face flushed and Bryn burst out laughing.

Grinning, Hayley apologized, "I'm sorry, Logan, that didn't sound quite right. My mouth has a tendency to blurt things out before my head can measure the consequences and uh, head it off, in a manner of speaking." She shook her head at her own garbled explanation, but continued on gamely. "What I meant to say is you're tall and when you shook my hand I noticed how large your hands are and—I'm going to stop right there before I get myself into any more trouble!"

Logan returned her grin. "I understand perfectly." He put his arm around Bryn and told her, "You were right, I like her."

Hayley heaved a heartfelt sigh of relief. "Whew!"

Logan laughed. "Come on, let's get your stuff in the house and get you settled."

Chapter Ten

ജ

Later that night, Bryn and Logan were relaxing in the den, after sharing a meal with Hayley, Clare and Brian at O'Neal's.

Hayley had retired to bed, the combination of travel and the late night having finally caught up with her. Despite her night owl habits she was sound asleep.

Logan had persuaded Bryn, without too much trouble that tonight would be a good night for their first run together. With that in mind, they passed some time in the den, content with each other's company as they gave Hayley time to settle in and get to sleep.

Logan's hands began to wander, one settling on her stomach, rubbing suggestively, the other cupping the full globe of one breast, causing her to wiggle as she leaned back against him.

"You're dangerous," she told him, placing her hands over his to still his movements. "It seems so strange to think there was a time that I avoided you like the plague. Now you're familiar, and so very beloved."

She angled her head back and their lips met in a deep, soul-searing kiss.

"As are you, my sweet little bitch," he murmured against her lips.

"Hey!" Bryn protested.

"Well…you are a female werewolf, sweetheart," Logan explained, as he nibbled her earlobe, causing a quick shudder of pleasure.

"Speaking of bitch," Bryn changed the subject, "has anyone heard from Lillian or Reece?"

"No. I imagine Reece is still ah, impressing his new position on Lillian," Logan quipped with a laugh.

Bryn chuckled. "Is that what you call it?"

"Oh yeah," Logan replied. "And whether he's behind her or in front of her, he'll definitely be the man on top." He returned to nuzzling Bryn's ear, his tongue tracing the stylized whorls. "I've got a new position I'm eager to try with you," he teased.

Bryn's lips curved in a naughty smile. "And what might that be?" she asked, as her heart beat faster.

Logan whispered in her ear as Bryn's eyes grew wider.

"I've read about that, but you're so big, it wouldn't fit there, would it?" she asked, intrigued and apprehensive at the same time.

"With a lot of lube—which I bought today by the way—and a lot of patience, it'll fit." He massaged her shoulders soothingly. "We'll take it real slow and careful. Want to try when we get back?"

Seriously considering, Bryn nodded her consent. "I've been curious about that," she admitted.

"That's another thing I love about you," Logan revealed, as he rose and pulled her into his arms. "There's always something going on in that busy brain of yours." He kissed her forehead, her nose, and then her lips. "Are you ready to go?"

Bryn nodded with a smile of anticipation. Her first time outside as a wolf. She almost trembled with the excitement.

Logan took her hand and they walked silently through the house into the kitchen, and let themselves out the back door. The moon was almost full, an ethereal, silvery disk in the midnight sky. They walked across the lawn and followed the path for a short distance before stopping to undress.

They regarded each other intently as they disrobed. Their eyes glowed and sparked with mutual excitement. Bryn could see the hard bulge of Logan's cock as it strained against his as yet unfastened jeans. A low rumbling growl stirred Logan's throat as Bryn revealed her breasts, the nipples pinched and distended in the cool night air.

Their heart and breathing rates sped as they quickly completed the task. Struggling to stick with their plan instead of dropping to the ground and taking each other, they stared into each other's eyes and simultaneously made the change.

The wolves faced each other, muzzles extended in greeting as their noses touched. The larger male whirled and began to run, veering away from the path to angle deeper into the woods. Without hesitation the smaller female followed.

Bryn was amazed. Her body worked with smooth, instinctive grace as she followed Logan. Effortlessly she ran, gliding with barely a rustle through the undergrowth. Her vision was so acute, she easily avoided anything that would trip the unaware.

Her nose twitched as the smells of the night drifted to her. She caught the rich, loamy smell of the earth under her feet as they stirred the rotting leaves of last year's fall, the tangy scent of pine and juniper from the evergreens. Particularly intriguing were the old and recent scents of deer, rabbit, quail and squirrel. The age-old need to hunt coursed through her veins like wine. Intoxicating, luring.

They ran until they reached the tall rock formation that gave the pack its name, Iron Tower. There, Logan ascended the leeward side with its gentle slope and stood, enfolded in the night and the gentle glow of moonlight. He raised his muzzle to the sky and howled out his joy of life and mate.

Bryn felt a quivering pull run through her taut body and she joined in his serenade. The free, wild sound filled the darkness and her heart pounded with exhilaration.

Logan rejoined her, licking her muzzle, sliding his body close to hers. His growl was filled with praise and satisfaction. He turned and again stretched out, running for the pure joy of it.

They ended their run at a stream-fed pond that lay in the woods behind the house. Logan changed form and Bryn easily followed suit.

She threw herself into his arms, laughing joyously as tears ran freely down her cheeks. "It's amazing, so amazing. I still can't believe it!"

"Was it all you hoped for, Bryn?" Logan asked.

"All and more!" She cupped his precious face in her hands. "Thank you, thank you, Logan. I love you so very much."

"No more than I love you, my sweet, wild woman." His lips captured hers as they sank down into the cool green grass by the pond. "My mate," he murmured against her lips. "Always."

His body covered hers, blanketing her in warmth as his hands and lips worshiped her. Bryn found herself staring into the golden amber glow of his eyes as he prepared to mount her. This was it, this was her dream. This man, her love and her life. This was her reward for trusting the wolf.

Epilogue

∾

Hayley was restless. She'd gone to bed and crashed for a couple of hours then woke abruptly, suddenly wide awake. The problem was, she was a night owl, and not used to going to bed so early. That, plus finding herself in an unfamiliar bed, had caused her to wake.

She went for the book she'd stashed in one of her bags, deciding a little romance and intrigue would be the very thing. As she crossed the floor, a board creaked underfoot. She paused and heard a scrabbling noise and some muffled laughter from down the hall. Apparently Bryn and Logan were just making their way to bed.

Hayley picked up the book, absently staring at it as her mind considered Bryn and Logan. Her smile was somewhat sad as she thought about her own lack of a love life. Why could she never meet the right guy? She focused on the book, and decided it wouldn't do. Quietly dressing, she walked softly down the hall, descended the stairs and made her way through the darkened house with the aid of the little flashlight she always carried on her keychain. The kitchen was just ahead, and if she remembered correctly there was a door that led out into the backyard.

As she let herself out, she breathed a sigh of relief and contentment. The night air was cool and fresh and she felt her spirits lift as she walked away from the house into the surrounding woods. The moon, a few days away from being full, rode high in the sky, making it easy for her to see the path that wound through the trees.

Hayley wandered slowly, no destination in mind. She'd always had a good sense of direction and felt at ease with nature. As she followed the path, she heard the soft splash of water in the distance.

Spotting the reflective glint of moonlight, she moved forward until she entered a clearing where a shallow pool of water was fed by a trickling stream. A smile lit her face as she walked to the edge of the pond. Kneeling, she trailed her fingers in the clear water. It was warm.

She gave the water a speculative look and then checked the surrounding area. Deciding to go for it, she quickly began to peel out of her clothes and, naked, stepped into the welcoming water.

She didn't see the pair of eyes that glowed with a bluish-green incandescence as they watched her lower herself into the pool.

The water was deep enough that she could swim, which she did, taking a few laps around its circumference. Wearying of that exercise, she flipped over on her back and floated, admiring the clear night sky with its moon and myriad stars all shining so brightly. Her body was so relaxed, she stifled a yawn as she found herself missing the bed she'd left not so long ago. With a sigh, she paddled to the edge of the pond and stood, walking from the water.

Hayley was unaware of the picture she presented as the water sluiced from her body, leaving it pale and shimmering under the moonlight. Her hair, slicked back, revealed the pure, lovely features of her face. Tall and lithe, her curves were full and firm. Bounteous breasts were topped by pink nipples that had hardened in the cool night air. A trim waist accentuated her generous hips and the sleek curve of taut buttocks. Below her slightly rounded belly, the nest of curls that graced her mound was pale and glistened with water from the pool. Her legs were long and curvaceous, from the tops of her shapely thighs to her slim, arched feet.

Reaching her clothes, she bent to retrieve her shirt and began to dry herself. A slight rustling sound caught her attention and she searched the darkness until her eyes found the wolf.

It stood with an air of calm majesty not twenty feet away. Hayley froze in surprise. A slight frisson of fear tightened her belly, until she remembered all the things she had read about wolves. One researcher in particular had said that wolves did not commonly attack humans and that during her study of them, the wolves, especially the males, had been curious about her and had often spent hours near her, seemingly studying her as she'd studied them.

Hayley strove to relax her tightened muscles as she admired the wolf. Its fur was thick and sleek, mostly black, lightening toward the chest, underbelly and legs. It seemed huge, although she had nothing to compare it with, never having seen a wolf before. And its eyes... Were they glowing? Surely it was a reflection of the moonlight off the water, she mused. Not sure what color eyes wolves usually had, she found the blue-green quite remarkable.

A wisp of night air blew across her skin, causing her to shiver. "I hope you don't mind," she told the wolf softly, "but I've got to move. I don't have any fur, you know, and it's a little chilly here with no clothes on."

In answer the wolf cocked his head, then sat, staring at her expectantly.

"Guess that means it's okay," Hayley muttered, as she carefully, with smooth easy movements, dressed herself.

All the while, the wolf watched with interest.

Slipping into her shoes, she faced the wolf. "Well, it was nice meeting you," she offered, "but I have to go. Hope you enjoyed the show."

In answer the wolf's mouth opened, his tongue lolling out in a large canine grin.

A suspicious frown crossed Hayley's face. "Did anyone ever tell you you were strange?" she asked, then admitted, "But very beautiful. Thank you for keeping me company. Maybe we'll meet again some time."

She backed away a few steps, just to see if there was any objection. When the wolf made no move, she turned and followed the trail back to the house. Slipping quietly into the kitchen, she locked the door and crept upstairs to her room, quickly changing and sliding back into bed.

Safe, warm and pleasantly sleepy, Hayley began to drift away until the haunting howl of a wolf pierced the night's quiet. She listened to the sound with awe as a shiver slid down her spine.

Just down the hall, Logan and Bryn both listened to the howl.

"Jace," Logan identified.

"What's he doing?" Bryn asked with a sleepy yawn.

Logan hugged her to him. "Probably just out for a run."

"Mmm," Bryn murmured, as she snuggled in and went to sleep.

Logan lay awake and listened to a second rolling howl. He'd heard Hayley return earlier from her moonlight ramble. He lay quietly, speculating upon the possibilities...

Enjoy These Excerpts From:

Lions and Tigers and Bears

LION EYES

"Will you be back for lunch?"

He didn't want to acknowledge the tinge of hopefulness in her eyes, and knew that any normal man wouldn't even notice it. But he wasn't quite normal and he also couldn't ignore it. She wanted to see him again today, and he wanted to see her again just as badly. "Do you want me to be?"

She blinked, but then said nonchalantly, "That's your call. I was thinking about picking up some Chinese, and they always give me enough for two."

He laughed, recalling the struggles she'd had the last time they'd shared Chinese. "You going to try to eat with chopsticks again?"

Her full lower lip pushed out in a pout, while her eyes gleamed with amusement. "I was thinking about it."

"Then consider it a date. There's nothing quite as entertaining as watching you try to get those things in your mouth with the food intact." Nothing short of trying to get something else in her mouth, that is. His tongue seemed as good as option as any, he thought when her lower lip pulled back in.

Though he knew how bad an idea it was to stand here and ogle her mouth, Kevin couldn't pull his attention away. Her lips shimmered as if she wore lip gloss, and he wondered if it were the flavored variety.

What would she taste like? Feel like beneath him? What sounds would she make when he slipped into her body and filled his hands with her generous breasts?

Liddy's tongue came out, a slip of pink dampening her lips, and his breathing heightened. With that slight lick, he knew she would taste better than any woman or female he'd ever kissed. She would taste like he would never be able to get enough.

It was the biggest reason he shouldn't reach out to her, shouldn't bend his head, but he found himself doing both, found himself watching her pupils dilate until her eyes were almost completely black. He found himself savoring the moment, and then he found himself cursing it when Liddy stepped back, away from his touch.

She took another step back and looked at the lions. "Yeah, um, so I'll see you at noon then, right?"

If he had any sense, he would say no, that he just remembered another meeting. Something about her obliterated his logic, though.

"Count on it," Kevin said, already anticipating the next time he would see her, when she'd be fighting to get the chopsticks in her mouth, and he'd been fighting himself to stop from imagining those sticks were something else entirely.

TIGER EYE

Zinsa engaged the parking brake and shut off the roaring engine of the old truck she had used to convey supplies and patients from her clinic to the makeshift site at the nature preserve. The door creaked when she opened it, and the muggy air settled on her like a shroud. During the drive over bumpy terrain, having the window down had given the illusion of cool air circulating, but she couldn't fool herself any longer. Even the buzzing flies seemed lethargic.

She slid from the truck, letting gravity carry her to the ground. As always, she made a mental note to install a step on the truck, but knew she probably never would. The value of the hulk of metal didn't warrant the investment. Besides, she thought with a small grin, the weight of the addition might destabilize the rusty bolts holding together the wreck on wheels.

The door groaned again when she slammed it, the window vibrating in the frame. Zinsa ignored the racket while simultaneously wondering how anyone unaccustomed to the truck could take no notice of all the noise. She had expected someone at the preserve's headquarters to come out to investigate, but as the dust settled, no one stepped out of the complex of wooden buildings that formed the offices and sleeping quarters of the employees.

"Hello?" she called. Receiving no reply, she moved away from the truck toward the entrance of the clinic, hoping to find someone available to help unload. She and the patients had managed to pack up everything from the clinic, but most were ill and worn out from the trip. It wasn't advisable to have the older patients lifting heavy boxes, which left only her, but she wasn't looking forward to doing all the work alone.

Stepping into the clinic caused a shiver to race down her spine. Not from the air circulated by multiple fans, but from the sight through the open office door of a man hunched over his desk, logging an entry into a ledger. His blond hair was a perfect foil for his dark tan, and the lightly curling locks made her fingers itch to run through them.

Surprised by her reaction, Zinsa walked to the doorway, composing her expression before clearing her throat. He jerked at the sound, and she said, "Sorry if I startled you, Dr. Hayden. I'm Zinsa Senghor. Manu might have mentioned..."

He nodded. Beyond a quicksilver flash of some inscrutable emotion in his green eyes, his expression was bland. "Yes. Would you like a tour?"

Zinsa walked closer to him, stopping before a large fan to pull her sticky tank top away from her skin, letting the artificial breeze waft over her. She sighed with contentment at the sensation, barely forcing herself to turn away to answer the vet. "Sure, but I need to get the patients in first, along with supplies. Care to give me a hand?"

After a brief hesitation, he nodded. "Of course." His chair squeaked when he pushed away from the basic desk.

Her eyes widened as he stood up straight. He was the tallest man she had ever seen. Surely he stood at least six-and-a-half feet. With his height, it wouldn't have been unwarranted to expect him to be bulging with muscles, but he had a trim physique. This was a man unafraid of physical labor, but not one who wasted hours honing his body to its maximum potential. Her mouth watered as he walked toward her and she swallowed, wishing he didn't have the kind of frame she found appealing.

Most of all, she wished she didn't feel this sensation that made her tingle, as if she had been struck by lightning. Was it the family gift—or curse, depending on how one looked at it? Was she finally experiencing the thing her father had described, had promised she would find someday? After thirty-two years, she had assumed it would never happen to her. It couldn't be happening now. With setting up a makeshift practice and seeing to her patients here instead of at her own clinic, she didn't have time for distractions.

At least, not right away, she thought with a mischievous grin as she turned to lead the way to her truck. Give her a couple of days, and he would be fair game. She would discover if what she felt was just instant attraction or something more.

HIDDEN HEART

"Do you always snoop through other people's personal property?"

She gasped and started guiltily. The question came from behind her, expressed in a deep voice, a silky growl that sent a shiver coursing down her spine—a shiver that unexpectedly caused her nipples to pinch tight.

"I'm sorry," she replied breathlessly, turning the pages back to their original position. "The sketchbook was open and the pictures were so beautiful." She rose and turned to face the speaker. "I just..." She stopped cold, her mouth open.

Standing before her, larger than life, was a flannel-clad God.

Tall herself, Lindy felt dwarfed by his presence. Her gaze slowly traveled the length of his six-foot-six-inch frame. Dressed in hiking boots and worn, faded jeans, with a tucked-in, dark blue flannel shirt, his clothing only served to emphasize the hard-muscled body beneath. His sleeves were rolled up to just below the elbow, and his forearms—lightly sprinkled with dark hair, and wrapped with a few prominent veins—were well defined. His hands were large, the fingers long and tapered and his skin was dark, not just tan, but brown, a rich, deep color that radiated warmth.

Lindy's heart actually fluttered when her gaze reached his face. The planes and hollows were precisely sculpted, on the verge of being hawk-like, yet softened by an unknown ancestor. His face was framed by black hair pulled severely back and bound by a leather tie. His eyes were dark, almost black, two pools of coffee that should have promised heat and stimulation, but now were hard and cold. His full lips were taut, his ire thinning them.

A dark brow rose. "You just...what?" he asked sarcastically.

Lindy blinked at his tone, attraction suddenly replaced by rising irritation. "Look, I'm sorry. No, I don't normally snoop through other people's belongings, but the book was out and open. I have to assume if it was private it wouldn't have been left where anyone could see it. Can we start over? I'm Lindy Timberlane." She stepped forward and held out her hand.

It was rudely ignored. "I know who you are, Miss Timberlane, and I may as well tell you that I don't approve of your being here." The irritable hunk moved passed her and leaned down to gather his papers.

Lindy couldn't help following the fluid movement of his body, her eyes widening at the sight of his hard, tight ass and how it moved under the taut fabric of his jeans when he bent over. She quickly snapped her eyes upward as he straightened and turned, pausing for a moment to study her. She felt her cheeks slowly begin to heat.

Those exquisite lips tightened again and sparks lit the depths of his dark eyes. "We're doing serious work here.

We're not here to guide some wealthy dilettante on a camping trip."

"I am not a wealthy dilettante! I work for a living, Mister...?"

"Kutter, Rafe Kutter."

"Mr. Kutter. I didn't donate money to curry any special favors. I didn't ask to come—I was invited."

"Yes, I know. And it was an invitation that was issued in spite of my disapproval. I was outvoted by the rest of the team. They seem to believe that your favor *needs* to be curried or the gravy train will halt."

Lindy gaped at him in disbelief. "Has anyone ever told you how obnoxious you are?"

Enjoy An Excerpt From:

WEATHER BALLOONS MAKE ROTTEN SEX TOYS

Available through Cerridwen Press

Unemployed scholar Annabelle du Fouet lived a quiet life until her Uncle Henry disappeared, leaving behind a mountain of kinky porn. Ordered by her Aunt Ruth to get rid of it, Annabelle decided to study the books, magazines and videos, hoping to understand Uncle Henry's secret life.

Then Annabelle made a decision that changed her life — to write the world's first research report on all things kinky. And she would do it from the inside. As Mistress Dominique, Annabelle plunged into the murky world of kink and changed it forever. Mostly for the worse, as it turned out. Follow Mistress Dominique's adventures as she:

— Destroys a kinky party by filling a house with smelly green foam.

— Causes a gigantic submissive known as Crazy Morty to terrorize a trailer park.

— Starts a riot that sends the chairwoman of the Savvy Seeders garden club to a psychiatric hospital.

— Leads a band of enraged ponygirls to attack the Rocking Robins bird club.

— Helps a drunken kinky clown traumatize a women's religious studies group.

And much more!

Through Annabelle's historical research, you will learn why Vikings were kinky but not as kinky as the ancient Egyptians. You will discover why the man who invented golf also invented an implement found in dungeons everywhere, and how a man named Thomas Edison (but not that Edison) nearly blew up a town by inventing the world's first electric kinky device. You will meet people with a fetish for pirate outfits, a man who wears an owl suit, and people who pretend to be elderly in order to cause scenes in bookstores.

Be warned though—while this in-depth research document contains frank discussions of sexual deviations, its history and the people who participate in it, there are no actual sexual encounters described. Really. Please! Annabelle is a professional and this was all done in the name of science.

Note: This book was previously released at Ellora's Cave Publishing.

INSPIRATION FROM UNCLE HENRY

It was a year ago that Uncle Henry disappeared. He just didn't come home one day and no one has heard from him since. My heart goes out to dear Aunt Ruth, who immediately went into hysterics. She cried not one tear over losing her beloved spouse of some thirty-five years. Instead, she spent her days smiling and laughing as though she were the happiest woman in the world. We begged her to get counseling but she only grinned and went on about how wonderful life had become. Poor woman.

Not long after Uncle Henry vanished, Aunt Ruth called and asked me to come over and sort through his belongings. "I want his shit out of here," she told me, "but I don't want to touch any of that slimy rat bastard's crap myself. I need you to take care of it."

Of course, it was the hysteria making her talk about her soul mate that way. Although I did not relish the idea of going through Uncle Henry's personal things, my heart went out to dear Aunt Ruth and I knew I had to help. Besides, I needed something to occupy me. My efforts to find employment as a professional researcher had been, to say the least, mysteriously unsuccessful, despite the fact that I hold a Ph.D. in Sociology from Indiana University and had once helped my faculty advisor create the index for one of her many scholarly books.

Armed with many empty boxes, I went to my aunt's home where she met me at the door with a radiant smile. The doctor must have given her tranquilizers to ease her pain, I thought, making a mental note to go along with whatever Aunt Ruth wanted, lest the hysterics recur.

"What do you think?" Aunt Ruth asked, pointing to her head. She'd changed her hair color from a mousey brown to a brilliant red, styled in a dramatic upsweep. She'd also started wearing makeup, with heavy blue eyeshadow, thick false eyelashes and bright red lipstick, all of which clashed with the tight purple flowered dress she'd wedged her chubby body into.

"Um, it's very nice," I lied, trying not to upset her delicate mental state.

Pointing a pudgy finger at Uncle Henry's den, Aunt Ruth gave me orders. "Pack it all up and burn it. Just set fire to it and stomp on the ashes. Put a wooden stake through it all. Pour acid on it. I don't care."

Lugging a suitcase from her bedroom, Aunt Ruth told me she was leaving the house in my care while she vacationed in the Bahamas. She stopped to primp in front of the hallway mirror then kissed her reflection, leaving a red lip print.

A car horn tooted in the driveway. "Antonio is right on time," Aunt Ruth beamed. Grabbing the suitcase, she hauled it to the door where Antonio waited. He was a short, thin man with greasy black hair and a pencil moustache, wearing tight pants and a shirt unbuttoned almost to the navel. Aunt Ruth said he was some sort of massage therapist who'd been treating her bad back. The young man embraced her warmly and whispered something in her ear, making Aunt Ruth giggle.

As Antonio hauled the suitcase to the car, Aunt Ruth gave me another gleaming smile. "I'll be gone for quite a long time, Annabelle. Do take care of the house for me like a good girl and don't forget to clear Henry's wretched things out of here." After giving me a loving peck on the cheek, poor distraught Aunt Ruth strode away, humming a tune to herself.

As the roar of Antonio's sports car faded in the distance, I looked sadly around the house once so full of love and gaiety, and now filled with the gloom of a wonderful marriage brought down in its prime. With a heavy heart, I began the task of removing Uncle Henry's belongings from his former home.

Bookshelves lined Uncle Henry's den, not surprising since he read voraciously. Glancing at the hundreds of books, I decided to pack them first and as I pulled the volumes from the shelves one-by-one, I couldn't help but glance at some of the titles. *The ABC's of BDSM*. Uncle Henry always did like word games. *Fun with Whips*. Obviously, some sort of cookbook about dessert toppings. *Leather and Loving It*. I remembered Aunt Ruth going on about how Uncle Henry was a "leather freak" and how he liked to hang out with his "sick friends". Knowing Uncle

Henry, he probably liked to make craft items for friends who were in the hospital.

As I continued packing, I noticed a theme. Many of the books featured scantily clad women on the dust jackets and some had covers showing what appeared to be men dressed as women, always with a stern woman standing nearby, holding a whip. As I am not as naive as some people think, I'm aware some men like to dress in female clothing but the presence of the whip-wielding women puzzled me. Perhaps the men in the pictures had stolen the clothing from the women, who used the whips to ensure the return their belongings. Using a whip seemed a drastic measure but as any woman knows, clothes are very expensive.

As explicit as the books were, they were tame compared to the magazines stored in the back of Uncle Henry's closet. All of them had extremely graphic covers, usually featuring menacing leather-clad women engaged in mean-spirited activities at the expense of apparently helpless men. They (the magazines, not the men) had exotic titles: *Leather Bitches from Hell, Goddess Betty and Her Amazon Army, Made Into a Maid,* on and on it went, all with the same general theme.

Later still, I discovered a cache of videotapes hidden behind a row of encyclopedias. They were just as explicit as the magazines, judging from the covers. *Genitals Prefer Blondes, Attack of the Bloodthirsty She-Devils, Whipped Into Shape,* and *Mister Chipmunk Gets Some Wood,* were just a few I saw, although that last title may well have been a children's video.

It took quite a few boxes to get all of Uncle Henry's materials packed away. When I finished, my spirits felt as empty as the den but I didn't have time to brood because I had to figure out what to do with everything I'd amassed. It seemed a shame to throw away Uncle Henry's things, weird as they might be, so I hired a man to truck them to my home, where I had them placed in my ample basement storage room.

Weeks went by. I heard little from Aunt Ruth, save for the occasional postcard from the Caribbean. Obviously, her emotional wounds still festered because many of her postcards made little sense, like this one:

Dearest Annabelle,

Having a splendid time! Last night I did a sixty-nine with Antonio that went on for HOURS. Later I even let him go in my back door, if you know what I mean, wink wink. I love that man's tool so much!

Much Love,

Aunt Ruth

I didn't know much about Antonio but with the talk of back doors and tools, I figured he must be a handyman of some sort. Perhaps they had rented a cottage that needed repairs. Anyway, I knew that even though Aunt Ruth needed desperately to talk about Uncle Henry, it must have been too painful to do so, since she never mentioned him in any of her postcards. Such a sad thing...

After the excitement involving my aunt and uncle, life settled into a routine once again but I found myself often drifting into a reverie, thinking about the odd materials packed away in my basement. Something about the books, magazines and videos intrigued me, despite my initial discomfort with their content. Obviously, Uncle Henry wasn't alone in his strange interests. Since he was able to amass such a large collection of materials, there must be others very much like him.

My intellectual curiosity finally got the best of me one evening, so I went to the basement and opened a box at random. Sitting in an old recliner that had long ago been relegated downstairs, I started to read some of Uncle Henry's books and magazines. Perhaps knowing something of his interests would enable me to know him better. Maybe I could even figure out what caused his sudden disappearance.

Before long, my scholarly instincts rose to the surface and I found myself eagerly consuming the contents of box after box, exulting in the process of learning. However, I must admit what I read appalled me, at least at first. Why would women want to treat men so horribly, beat them with whips, tie them up, force them to wear women's clothing? Adding to my confusion was the arcane lingo used in the books and magazines. With my extensive background in linguistics, however, I was soon able to grasp the meaning of such terms as *bitch goddess, golden showers* (ick!), *rim job* (ick! ick!) and *scat* (triple ick!).

I spent many evenings in that recliner, pouring over the vast array of materials at hand. As time went on, I realized I'd become obsessed with "the world of kink," as I came to think of it. I gave up all other activities in order to further my research, too busy either reading about kink or watching it on one of Uncle Henry's many videos.

I began to receive phone calls from my friends at the canasta club, wondering if I was okay. The chairwoman of the Harold Leipnitz Film Appreciation Society came to visit, wanting to know why I'd missed so many meetings, especially the one where it was my turn to bring coffeecake. That particular visit did not go well, as I had absent-mindedly answered the door holding a copy of *Lactating Dommes* magazine, the cover featuring a large-breasted woman squirting milk on a bound and gagged male slave. From her chilly reaction, I knew it would be some time before the Leipnitz Society welcomed me back.

After weeks of serious study, I was surprised to find one evening that I had exhausted every box of Uncle Henry's kinky collection. Strangely enough, I felt a letdown, knowing I had nothing left to study.

Or did I?

Why an electronic book?

We live in the Information Age—an exciting time in the history of human civilization, in which technology rules supreme and continues to progress in leaps and bounds every minute of every day. For a multitude of reasons, more and more avid literary fans are opting to purchase e-books instead of paper books. The question from those not yet initiated into the world of electronic reading is simply: *Why?*

1. ***Price.*** An electronic title at Ellora's Cave Publishing and Cerridwen Press runs anywhere from 40% to 75% less than the cover price of the exact same title in paperback format. Why? Basic mathematics and cost. It is less expensive to publish an e-book (no paper and printing, no warehousing and shipping) than it is to publish a paperback, so the savings are passed along to the consumer.

2. ***Space.*** Running out of room in your house for your books? That is one worry you will never have with electronic books. For a low one-time cost, you can purchase a handheld device specifically designed for e-reading. Many e-readers have large, convenient screens for viewing. Better yet, hundreds of titles can be stored within your new library—on a single microchip. There a variety of e-readers from different manufacturers. You can also read e-books on your PC or laptop computer. (Please note that Ellora's

Cave does not endorse any specific brands. You can check our websites at www.ellorascave.com or www.cerridwenpress.com for information we make available to new consumers.)

3. *Mobility.* Because your new e-library consists of only a microchip within a small, easily transportable e-reader, your entire cache of books can be taken with you wherever you go.

4. ***Personal Viewing Preferences.*** Are the words you are currently reading too small? Too large? Too… ANNOYING? Paperback books cannot be modified according to personal preferences, but e-books can.

5. ***Instant Gratification.*** Is it the middle of the night and all the bookstores near you are closed? Are you tired of waiting days, sometimes weeks, for bookstores to ship the novels you bought? Ellora's Cave Publishing sells instantaneous downloads twenty-four hours a day, seven days a week, every day of the year. Our webstore is never closed. Our e-book delivery system is 100% automated, meaning your order is filled as soon as you pay for it.

Those are a few of the top reasons why electronic books are replacing paperbacks for many avid readers.

As always, Ellora's Cave and Cerridwen Press welcome your questions and comments. We invite you to email us at Comments@ellorascave.com or write to us directly at Ellora's Cave Publishing Inc., 1056 Home Avenue, Akron, OH 44310-3502.

THE
⚥ ELLORA'S CAVE ⚥
LIBRARY

Stay up to date with Ellora's Cave Titles in
Print with our Quarterly Catalog.

TO RECIEVE A CATALOG,
SEND AN EMAIL WITH YOUR NAME
AND MAILING ADDRESS TO:

CATALOG@ELLORASCAVE.COM

OR SEND A LETTER OR POSTCARD
WITH YOUR MAILING ADDRESS TO:

CATALOG REQUEST
c/o ELLORA'S CAVE PUBLISHING, INC.
1056 HOME AVENUE
AKRON, OHIO 44310-3502

ELLORA'S CAVEMEN

LEGENDARY TAILS

Try an e-book for your immediate
reading pleasure or order these titles in print from

WWW.ELLORASCAVE.COM

COMING TO A BOOKSTORE NEAR YOU!

ELLORA'S CAVE

Bestselling Authors Tour

UPDATES AVAILABLE AT

www.EllorasCave.com

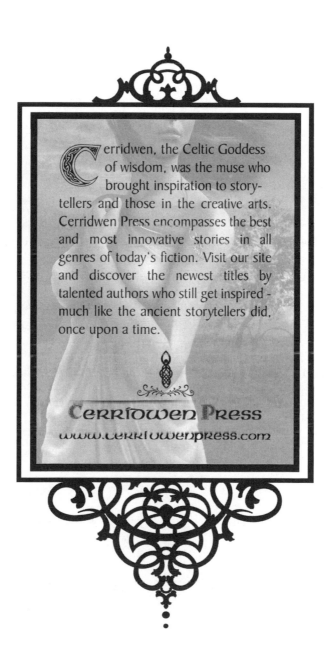

erridwen, the Celtic Goddess of wisdom, was the muse who brought inspiration to storytellers and those in the creative arts. Cerridwen Press encompasses the best and most innovative stories in all genres of today's fiction. Visit our site and discover the newest titles by talented authors who still get inspired - much like the ancient storytellers did, once upon a time.

Cerridwen Press

www.cerridwenpress.com

Discover for yourself why readers can't get enough of the multiple award-winning publisher

Ellora's Cave.

Whether you prefer e-books or paperbacks,

be sure to visit EC on the web at
www.ellorascave.com

for an erotic reading experience that will leave you breathless.